"I need to return to Zeena Sahra. The cancellation of my engagement will have long-reaching consequences for our country."

Feeling unaccountably bereft at the thought of Sayed's abandonment, Liyah nevertheless nodded. "I understand."

"Good. It is unfortunate you will not be able to work out your notice, but it is fortuitous that you already made your plans to leave."

"What? Why won't I work out my notice?"

"I've told you, we must leave for Zeena Sahra immediately."

"You said you had to leave."

He gave her a look that said she wasn't following him. "Naturally you must come with me."

"Why?"

"You may carry my child."

"But we don't know that."

"And until we do, you stay with me."

Step into the opulent glory of the world's most elite hotel, where the clients are the impossibly rich and exceptionally famous.

Whether you're in America, Australia, Europe or Dubai our doors will always be open...

Welcome to

The Chatsfield

Synonymous with style, sensation...and scandal!

For years, the children of Gene Chatsfield—global hotel entrepreneur—have shocked the world's media with their exploits. But no longer! When Gene appoints a new CEO, Christos Giatrakos, to bring his children into line, little does he know what he is starting.

Christos's first command scatters the Chatsfields to the farthest reaches of their international holdings—from Las Vegas to Monte Carlo, Sydney to San Francisco.... But will they rise to the challenge set by a man who hides dark secrets in his past?

Let the games begin!

Your room has been reserved, so check in to enjoy all the passion and scandal we have to offer.

Enter your reservation number:

00106875

at

www.TheChatsfield.com

The Chatsfield

Sheikh's Scandal Lucy Monroe

Playboy's Lesson Melanie Milburne

Socialite's Gamble Michelle Conder

Billionaire's Secret Chantelle Shaw

Tycoon's Temptation Trish Morey

Rival's Challenge Abby Green

Rebel's Bargain Annie West

Heiress's Defiance Lynn Raye Harris

Eight volumes to collect—you won't want to miss out!

Lucy Monroe

—

Sheikh's Scandal

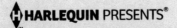

HARLEQUIN PRESENTS®

Recycling programs
for this product may
not exist in your area.

ISBN-13: 978-0-373-13716-9

SHEIKH'S SCANDAL

First North American Publication 2014

Copyright © 2014 by Harlequin Books S.A.

Special thanks and acknowledgment are given to Lucy Monroe for her contribution to The Chatsfield series.

Printed in U.S.A.

www.Harlequin.com

All about the author...
Lucy Monroe

Award-winning and bestselling author **Lucy Monroe** sold her first book in September 2002 to the Harlequin Presents® line. That book represented a dream that had been burning in her heart for years—the dream to share her stories with readers who love romance as much as she does. Since then she has sold more than thirty books to three publishers and hit national bestseller lists in the U.S. and England, but what has touched her most deeply since selling that first book are the reader letters she receives. Her most important goal with every book is to touch a reader's heart, and when she hears she's done that it makes every night spent writing into the wee hours of the morning worth it.

She started reading Harlequin Presents® books when she was very young and discovered a heroic type of man between the covers of those books...an honorable man, capable of faithfulness and sacrifice for the people he loves. Now married to what she terms her "alpha male at the end of a book," Lucy believes there is a lot more reality to the fantasy stories she writes than most people give credit for. She believes in happy endings that are really marvelous beginnings, and that's why she writes them. She hopes her books help readers to believe a little, too...just as romance did for her so many years ago.

She really does love to hear from readers and responds to every email. You can reach her by emailing lucymonroe@lucymonroe.com.

Other titles by Lucy Monroe available in ebook:

MILLION DOLLAR CHRISTMAS SURPRISE
PRINCE OF SECRETS *(By His Royal Decree)*
ONE NIGHT HEIR *(By His Royal Decree)*
NOT JUST THE GREEK'S WIFE

CHAPTER ONE

NOT EASILY IMPRESSED, Liyah Amari very nearly stopped to gawp upon entering the Chatsfield London for the first time.

Flagship of the Chatsfield family's hotel empire, the lodging preferred by Europe's elite was magnificent.

San Francisco's property where her mother had worked since before Liyah's birth was beautiful, but nothing compared to the opulence of this hotel. From the liveried doormen to the grandeur of the ballroom-size lobby, she felt as if she'd stepped into a bygone era of luxury.

A decidedly frenetic air of anticipation and preparation was at odds with the elegant surroundings, though. One maid rushed through the lobby—which Liyah was certain was anything but a normal occurrence—while another polished the walnut banisters of the grand staircase.

It looked like an impromptu but serious meeting was happening near the concierge desk. The desk reception staff were busy with the phone and computer, respectively, checking in an attractive elderly couple.

"Welcome to the Chatsfield London, Mr. and Mrs. Michaels. Here is your room key," the young man said, "and here is your complimentary hospitality pack. We very much hope that you enjoy your stay."

Both staff were too busy to pay attention to who might be entering the hotel. Behind reception, Liyah saw a row of photographs depicting the Chatsfield London's staff. Something in her chest tightened as she caught the image of Lucilla Chatsfield staring back at her from within a frame.

One of the Chatsfield siblings Liyah admired and wished she could get to know, Lucilla was too far up the hotel's ranks for that to ever be likely.

A noise from behind her dragged her attention to where maintenance was replacing a bulb in the giant chandelier that cast the saffron walls with an elegant glow. Ecru moldings and columns added a tasteful but subtly lavish touch and the faint but lingering smell of fresh paint indicated they'd had a recent tidying up.

Liyah's sensible shoes made no noise as she crossed the black-and-white marble-tiled floor, heading directly for the elevator as she'd been instructed to do.

A man stepped in front of her. "May I help you find someone?"

His tone and expression were polite, but it had to be obvious to him that Liyah in her well-fitting but conservative black gabardine suit was not a guest at the Chatsfield.

"I have an appointment with Mrs. Miller." As was her usual habit, Liyah was fifteen minutes early for her meeting with the senior housekeeper.

The man's eyes lit up. "Oh, you must be the maid from Zeena Sahra."

No. That had been her mother. "I am familiar with Zeena Sahran culture, but I was born in America."

Liyah had been hired as a floor supervising chambermaid on the presidential level with special concierge services, just below the hotel's penthouse suites. With hospitality as well as housekeeping duties, she would be working in tandem with the concierge team in a new initiative designed to increase customer satisfaction.

It would be a much more satisfying job for Liyah than the one her mother had held for almost three decades and Hena would have approved wholeheartedly.

"Yes, of course. The elevator is right this way."

The man started walking. "I will have to key your access to the basement level."

"Thank you."

Liyah was still a few minutes early when she knocked on the senior housekeeper's office door.

"Enter," came from within.

Mrs. Miller was a tall, thin woman who wore a more severe version of Liyah's suit with a starched white blouse buttoned all the way up.

"I'm pleased you are here, Miss Amari, but I hope you've come prepared to begin work immediately," she said after the pleasantries were out of the way.

"Yes, of course."

"Good. Your concierge floor has been booked for the sheikh's harem." Mrs. Miller gave a disdainful sniff with the word *harem*.

"Excuse me? A sheikh from Zeena Sahra is coming to stay?" And he needed an *entire floor* for his harem?

No wonder they'd wanted to transfer her mother from the Chatsfield San Francisco.

"Yes, Sheikh bin Falah will be staying with us for two weeks. His fiancée will be joining him for the second one."

Liyah schooled the shock from her features. "Sheikh al Zeena, or Sheikh bin Falah al Zeena, but he would not be referred to as Sheikh bin Falah. To do so would cause offence."

Liyah wasn't sure about correcting her boss, but she assumed this sort of knowledge was why she'd been hired.

At least now she understood the need for her *expertise*. Not just a tribal sheikh but the crown prince of Zeena Sahra was coming to stay at the Chatsfield London.

Probably the single most gorgeous man alive, he could easily be an international playboy with a string of supermodels hanging on his arm. However, he had a reputation for being buttoned-down and focused entirely on his duties as emir of Zeena Sahra.

"I see. I'll make a note of it. I presume addressing him as Your Highness is acceptable."

"It is, though from what I have read, since Zeena Sahra is an emirate, he prefers the title of *emir*."

Mrs. Miller's mouth pursed. "Why didn't we know this?"

"It's a small thing, really."

"No," Mrs. Miller said sharply. "There's nothing small about this visit from the sheikh. Every detail must be seen to with absolute attention. If not, mistakes happen. Only last week someone wanted to send silk napkins to the Chatsfield Preitalle with the inscription 'Princess Maddie.' Can you believe it? For a royal wedding? This is why each detail *must* be perfect."

"I will do my best."

"Yes. In addition to your usual duties, for the duration of the sheikh's visit, you will also personally oversee the housekeeping staff for his suite and the adjoining rooms for his security people."

Nothing like being thrown in at the deep end, but Liyah didn't mind. She thrived on a challenge.

Nevertheless, it was a good thing Liyah had gotten her degree in hospitality management. It didn't hurt either that she'd cleaned rooms at the Chatsfield San Francisco every summer break through high school and college, not that her mother had encouraged Liyah to make her career there.

Quite the opposite, Hena had been adamant that her daughter *not* work for the Chatsfield. And now that she knew what she did, maybe Liyah understood that better.

After a somewhat harried orientation, during which staff members she met asked as many questions of Liyah about Zeena Sahra as she asked them about the Chatsfield London, she returned to her newly rented bedsit.

About the size of a college dorm room with an efficiency kitchen and miniscule bath tacked on, it was a far cry from the two-bedroom apartment with a balcony she'd shared with her mother in

San Francisco. An apartment she'd been only too happy to move out of when she got the floor supervisory position with the Chatsfield London.

The job offer was a brilliant coincidence that Liyah's mother would have called destiny. But then Hena Amari had had a romantic streak her daughter did not share.

Although her outlook on life was decidedly more pragmatic, once Liyah had seen the contents of her mother's safety-deposit box and read Hena's final letter, she'd known she had to come to England.

The new job had allowed her to do so without dipping too deeply into what was left from the proceeds of her mother's life insurance policy. The money had been welcome if entirely unexpected. The policy had been one of the many profound shocks Liyah had found in that safety-deposit box.

Shocks that had ultimately ended with her working for the Chatsfield London.

The hotel had been looking specifically for someone with knowledge of Zeena Sahran culture and hospitality norms. Ironically, they had contacted the San Francisco property's senior housekeeper, Stephanie Carter, in hopes of transferring Hena Amari.

With Hena's sudden death, Stephanie, knowing about Liyah, had suggested her instead. Even though Liyah had not worked for the Chatsfield San Francisco since the summer before her last year of university, her education and experience had made her uniquely eligible for a newly created position.

The irony that a job with the hotel would make it possible for her daughter to fulfill Hena's final wish was not lost on Liyah.

Liyah did not resent her mother's silence on any front, but only superb emotional control had allowed her to take one stunning revelation after another without cracking.

On the outside.

The most stunning revelation of all had been that the extremely wealthy English hotelier Gene Chatsfield was Liyah's biological father.

After years of seeing the exploits of his legitimate children in the tabloid press, Liyah found it nearly impossible to believe his blood ran through her veins. What did she, a woman who had worked hard for everything she had, have in common with this notorious, spoiled family?

She had an almost morbid curiosity to discover what kind of man raised his children to be so profligate while sending the most meager of stipends to Hena on Liyah's behalf.

The answer might lie in the very fact of Liyah's existence, the result of Gene's indulgence in numerous affairs with his hotel maids. Affairs that did *not* make it into the press.

Hena hadn't known about the hotelier's wife, much less his propensity for seducing the chambermaids, until after he left San Francisco and a pregnant Hena behind. It had all been in the final letter Hena had left Liyah.

She'd never told another soul the identity of Liyah's father. Hena's shame in the fact he'd been a married man colored the rest of her life and yet she'd written in her letter that Liyah needed to forgive him.

Hena had claimed that Gene Chatsfield was not a villain, not a demon, not even a very bad man. But he had been a man going through a very bad time. Her final request had been for Liyah to come to London and make herself known to her father.

Liyah would respect her mother's last wishes, but she was happy to have the opportunity to observe the man incognito—as an employee, not the daughter he'd never acknowledged.

Her uniform crisp, her long black hair caught in an impeccable bun, Liyah stood tucked away in a nook near the grand staircase. She'd been in London two weeks and working at the Chatsfield ten hectic days, but had yet to catch a glimpse of her father.

Word had come down that the Honorable
Sheikh Sayed bin Falah al Zeena was arriving
today, though. Liyah had no doubts her father
would be on hand to greet the sheikh personally.

One thing that had become patently obvious in
the past ten days: the sheikh's stay was incredibly important to the hotel, and even more significant to the Chatsfield's proprietor.

Apparently, in another ironic twist of fate,
Gene Chatsfield currently resided in the Chatsfield New York, leaving his new and highly
acclaimed CEO, Christos Giatrakos, alone to
handle operations from London. However, Gene
Chatsfield's arrival in London to *personally* oversee the emir's visit said it all.

Knowing how key this high-profile guest's
stay was to her father, Liyah was determined to
do her job well. When she made herself known
to Gene, there would be nothing to disappoint
him in *her* work ethic.

Her floor was in impeccable order, each of
the rooms to be occupied garnished with a crystal bowl of fruit and a vase of fragrant jasmine.
She'd arranged for a screen to be placed at the
elevator bank on her floor, as well, effectively
blocking the harem quarters from curious looks.

She'd made sure the sheikh's suite was simi-
larly taken care of. There was nothing to offend

and a great deal to appreciate in her setup of his rooms and the floor below.

Thoughts of her work faded as an older man walked with supreme confidence across the lobby. His air that of a man who owned all he surveyed, he acknowledged the numerous greetings by his employees with a regal tip of his head. Her father.

Stopping in front of the reception desk, he was clearly prepared to welcome the sheikh upon arrival.

Gray hair shot with silver, his blue eyes were still clear, his six-foot-one frame just slightly stooped. Garbed in a perfectly tailored Pierre Cardin suit, his shoes no doubt handmade, he looked like a man who would fit right in with the fabulously wealthy people his hotel catered to.

Gene smiled and said something to the head of desk reception. And all the air expelled from Liyah's lungs in a single whoosh.

She'd seen that smile in the mirror her whole life. His lips were thinner, but the wide smile above a slightly pointed chin? That was so familiar it made her heart ache.

His eyes were blue, hers were green—but their shape was the same. That hadn't been obvious in the publicity shots she'd seen of him.

She'd gotten her mother's honey-colored skin, oval face, small nose and arched brows, not to mention Hena's black hair and five-foot-five stature. Their mother-daughter connection had been obvious to anyone who saw them together.

Liyah had never considered she might also share physical traits with her father.

The resemblance wasn't overly noticeable by any means, but that smile? Undeniably like hers.

This man was her father.

Hit with the profundity of the moment, Liyah's knees went to jelly and she had to put her hand against the wall for stability.

Unaware of her father's moderate financial support and way too aware of the Amari rejection of any connection, Liyah had spent her life knowing of only one person in her family.

Hena Amari.

Her mom was the only Amari who had ever recognized Liyah as a member of that family. A family who had cast her out for her *disgrace*.

And since her mom's death, Liyah had been alone. In that moment, she realized that if this man accepted her—even into the periphery of his life—she wouldn't be alone any longer.

Her father's face changed, the smile shifting to something a lot tenser than the expression he'd worn only seconds before. He stood a little straighter, his entire demeanor more alert.

Liyah's gaze followed his, and for the second

time in as many minutes she went weak in the knees.

Surrounded by an impressive entourage and dressed in the traditional garb of a Zeena Sahran sheikh stood the most beautiful man Liyah had ever seen. Known for his macho pursuits and outlook, despite his supreme political diplomacy, the emir wouldn't appreciate the description, she was sure.

But regardless of...or maybe *because of* his over-six-foot height, square jaw and neatly trimmed, close-cropped facial hair, the sheikh's masculine looks carried a beauty she'd never before encountered.

No picture she'd ever seen did him justice. Two-dimensional imagery could never catch the reality of Sheikh Sayed bin Falah al Zeena's presence. Not his gorgeous looks or the leashed power that crackled in the air around him like electricity.

Nothing about the unadorned black *abaya* worn over Armani, burgundy *keffiyeh* on his head and black triple-stranded *egal* holding it in place expressed anything but conservative control. The Zeena Sahran color of royalty of the *keffiyeh* and three strands of the *egal,* rather than the usual two, subtly indicated his status as emir.

Wearing the traditional robe over a tailored designer suit with the head scarf implied supreme civilization. And yet, to her at least, it was obvious the blood of desert warriors ran in his veins.

The first melech of Zeena Sahra had won independence for his tribe—which later became the founding people of the emirate of Zeena Sahra—through bloody battles western history books often glossed over.

Inexplicably and undeniably drawn to the powerful man, Liyah's feet carried her forward without her conscious thought or volition. It was only when she stood mere feet from the royal sheikh that Liyah came to an abrupt, embarrassed stop.

It was too late, though.

Sheikh Sayed's espresso-brown gaze fell on her and remained, inquiry evident in the slight quirking of his brows.

Considered unflappable by all who knew her, Liyah couldn't think of a single coherent thing to say, not even a simple welcome before moving on.

No, she stood there, her body reacting to his presence in a way her mother had always warned Liyah about but she had never actually experienced.

Part of her knew that he was surrounded by the people traveling with him, the Chatsfield Hotel staff and even her father, but Liyah could only see the emir. Discussion around them was nothing more than mumbling to her ears.

The signature scent of the Chatsfield—a mix

of cedarwood, leather, white rose and a hint of lavender—faded and all she could smell was the emir's spicy cologne blending with his undeniable masculine scent.

Her nipples drew tight for no discernible reason, her heart rate increasing like it only did after a particularly challenging workout and her breath came in small gasps she did her best to mask with shallow inhales.

His expression did not detectably change, but something in the depths of his dark gaze told her she was not the only one affected.

"Sheikh al Zeena, this is Amari, our chambermaid floor supervisor in charge of the harem floor and your suite," the head of desk reception stepped in smoothly to say.

Being referred to by her last name was something Liyah was used to; meeting a crown prince was not.

However, her brain finally came back online and she managed to curl her right hand over her left fist and press them over her left breast. Bowing her head, she leaned slightly forward in a modified bow. "Emir. It is my pleasure to serve you and your companions."

Sayed had a wholly unacceptable and unprecedented reaction to the lovely chambermaid's words and actions.

His sex stirred, images of exactly *how* he would like her to serve him flashing through his mind in an erotic slide show of fantasies he was not aware of even having.

The rose wash over her cheeks and vulnerable, almost hungry expression in her green eyes told him those desires could be met, increasing his unexpected viscerally sexual reaction tenfold. Hidden by the fall of his *abaya,* his rapidly engorging flesh ached with unfamiliar need.

Sayed's status as a soon-to-be-married man, not to mention melech of his country, dictated he push the images aside and ignore his body's physical response, however. No matter how difficult he found doing so.

"Thank you, Miss Amari," Sayed said, his tone imperious by necessity to hide his reaction to her. He indicated the woman assigned to tend his domestic needs. "This is Abdullah-Hasiba. She will let you know of any requirements we may have. Should you have any questions, they can be taken directly to her, as well."

Miss Amari's beautiful green gaze chilled and her full lips firmed slightly, but nothing else in her demeanor indicated a reaction to his clear dismissal.

"Thank you, Your Highness." Dipping her head again in the tradition of his people, she then turned to his servant. "I look forward to working with you Miz Abdullah-Hasiba."

With another barely-there dip of her head, the much-too-attractive hotel employee did that thing well-trained servants were so good at and seemed to just melt away.

Sayed had a baffling and near-unstoppable urge to call her back.

CHAPTER TWO

STILL GRAPPLING WITH the fact she'd forgotten her father in the presence of the emir, Liyah knocked on Miz Abdullah-Hasiba's door.

She hadn't even taken the chance to meet Gene Chatsfield's eyes for the first time. How could she have missed such a prime opportunity?

She was here to observe her father and ultimately make herself known to him. Liyah had not come to the Chatsfield London to ogle a Zeena Sahran prince.

Aaliyah Amari did not *ogle* anyone.

The door in front of her swung open. The unexpectedness of it, even though she'd been the one to knock, further emphasized how disconnected from her normal self Liyah was.

Wearing a dark apricot *kameez* embroidered around the neck and wrists with pale yellow thread, the emir's personal housekeeper clasped her hands in front of her and bent her head forward. "Miss Amari, how may I be of service?"

"I wanted to make sure you and the emir's other female traveling companions have found your accommodations acceptable."

"Very much so." The older woman stepped back and indicated Liyah should enter her room. "Please, come in."

"I do not want to take you from your duties."

"Not at all. You must share a cup of tea with me."

With no polite way to decline, and frankly not inclined to do so, Liyah followed the other woman to the small sofa on the other side of the deluxe room. As much as it might bother her, Liyah could not deny her fascination with the emir.

At least, not to herself.

The Middle Eastern tea service Liyah had purchased on behalf of the hotel—along with the ones for the sheikh and his fiancée's suites—sat in the center of the oval coffee table.

Miz Abdullah-Hasiba poured the fragrant hot drink from the copper-and-glass pot into the short, narrow matching cups with no handles. "This is a treat."

"Yes?"

The housekeeper nodded with a smile. "Oh, yes. We do not travel with glassware as it is too easily broken."

"Naturally." Liyah waited for the housekeeper

to take a sip before following suit, enjoying the sweetened warm beverage and the bittersweet memories it evoked.

Her mom had insisted on beginning and ending each day with a cup of mint tea augmented by a touch of honey.

"Nevertheless, the Chatsfield is the first hotel on the emir's current European travel itinerary to have thought to provide the traditional tea service."

"They will only be found in your room, the emir's suite and that of his fiancée, I'm afraid."

The older woman smiled. "Your grasp of our culture is commendable. Most hotel staff would have put the tea set in the room for the emir's secretary."

Liyah did not shrug off the praise, but neither did she acknowledge it. She was more aware of the Zeena Sahran culture than the average Brit or American, but anyone observant would have taken note that the housekeeper had been booked in the most deluxe room beside the emir's fiancée's suite.

"His secretary is actually junior office staff, I believe," Liyah observed.

"She is. The emir follows the old ways. By necessity, his personal administrative assistant is Duwad, a male."

"Because your emir cannot work late hours in

his suite with a woman, married or otherwise," Liyah guessed.

"Precisely."

"So, this is a business trip?" Very little had been said in the media about the nature of the emir's current travel plans.

"For the most part. Melech Falah insisted Emir Sayed enjoy a final European tour as it were before taking on the mantle of full leadership of our country."

"The king intends to abdicate the throne to his son?" She'd read speculation to that effect, but nothing concrete.

"One might consider that a possible course of events after the royal wedding."

Liyah approved the other woman's carefully couched answer and did not press for anything more definite. "Our head of housekeeping was scandalized at the thought of booking a separate floor for a sheikh's harem."

"Ah. She assumed he would be bringing a bevy of belly dancers to see to his *needs,* no doubt."

"That may have been her understanding, yes." Liyah herself had assumed something similar, if not quite so fanciful when first told of the harem.

The Zeena Sahran housekeeper laughed softly. "Nothing so dramatic, I am afraid. The emir is ever mindful of his position as a betrothed man."

Not sure she believed that, but having very little practical experience with men and none at all with their sex drives, Liyah didn't argue. She did know the rooms she'd prepared had all been for different female staff members of the prince's entourage.

Most of the rooms that would ultimately be occupied were slated to house the emir's fiancée and her mostly female traveling companions. Her brother was supposed to be accompanying her, as well, and had booked a suite on the presidential level near the emir's.

Not quite as grand, it was nevertheless impressive accommodation.

After a surprisingly enjoyable visit with Hasiba—as she insisted on being called—in which the housekeeper managed to convey unspoken but clear reservations toward the future emira of Zeena Sahra, Liyah left for a meeting with the concierge.

He and his staff expected her input on a finalization of entertainment offerings to make to the sheikh over the next two weeks.

Liyah came out of the royal suite, pleased with the care the chambermaid assigned to the emir's rooms had taken.

The vases of purple iris—the official flower of Zeena Sahra—Liyah had ordered were fresh and perfectly arranged. The bowls with floating jasmine on either side of the candelabra on the formal dining table did not have a single brown spot on the creamy white blossoms.

The beds were all made without a single wrinkle and the prince's tea service was prepped for his late-afternoon repast.

She headed for the main elevator. While staff were encouraged to use the service elevator, she was not required to do so. The busiest time of day for housekeeping and maintenance usually coincided with light use on the guest elevators.

So, as she'd done at her hotel in San Francisco, Liyah opted to use them when she wasn't carrying towels or pushing a cleaning cart. Something she rarely had to do in her position as lead chambermaid, but not outside the realm of possibility.

The doors slid open with a quiet whoosh and Liyah's gaze was snagged by espresso-brown eyes.

The emir stared back, his expression a strange mixture of surprise and something else she had very little experience interpreting. "Miss Amari?"

"Emir Sayed." She dipped her head in acknowledgment of his status. "I was just checking on your suite."

"The service has been impeccable."

"I'm glad you think so. I'll be sure and pass

your kind words on to your suite's housekeeping staff."

He inclined his head in regal agreement she doubted he was even aware of.

She waited for him to step out of the elevator, but he did not move. His security detail had exited first with a smooth precision that came off as a deeply ingrained habit, followed by the emir's administrative assistant and the junior secretary.

They all waited, as well, for their sheikh to move.

Only he didn't.

He pressed a button and the doors started to close. "Are you coming?" His tone implied impatience.

Though she didn't know why. Her brain couldn't quite grasp what he was doing on the other side of the doorway. If he was going back down again, wouldn't his security be on the elevator with him?

One thing she did know: she wasn't about to commit the faux pas of joining the emir. "Oh, no. I'll just go to the service elevator."

"Do not be ridiculous." He reached out and grabbed her wrist, drawing shocked gasps from his staff and an imprecation in the Zeena Sahran dialect of Arabic from his personal bodyguard.

Liyah had little opportunity to take that in as she was pulled inexorably into the elevator through the shrinking gap between the heavy doors.

They closed behind her on another Arabic curse, this one much louder and accompanied by a shocked and clearly disapproving, *"Emir Sayed!"*

"Your Highness?"

"There is no reason for you to take another elevator."

"But your people…shouldn't you have waited for them?"

His elegant but strong fingers were still curled around her wrist and he showed no intention of letting her go. "I am not accustomed to being questioned in my actions by a servant."

The words were dismissive, his tone arrogant, even cold, but the look in his eyes wasn't. She'd never heard of brown fire before, but it was there in his gaze right now.

Hot enough to burn the air right from her lungs.

Nevertheless, her professional demeanor leaned toward dignified, not subservient. By necessity, she pulled the cool facade she'd per-fected early in life around her with comfortable familiarity.

"And I am not used to being manhandled by hotel guests." She stared pointedly at his hold on her wrist, expecting him to release her immediately.

It wasn't acceptable in the more conservative culture of Zeena Sahra for him to touch *any* single woman outside his immediate family—and that did not include cousins—much less one that was a complete stranger to him.

However, his hold remained. "This is hardly manhandling."

His thumb rubbed over her pulse point and Liyah had no hope of suppressing her shiver of reaction.

His heated gaze reflected confusion, as well. "I don't understand this."

He'd spoken in the dialect of his homeland, no doubt believing she wouldn't know what he was saying. She didn't disabuse him of the belief.

She couldn't. Words were totally beyond her.

For the first time in her life, she craved touch worse than dark chocolate during that most inconvenient time of the month.

"You are an addiction," he accused, his tone easy to interpret even if she hadn't spoken the Zeena Sahran dialect fluently.

Suddenly embarrassed, wondering if she'd done something to invite his interest and reveal her own, she pulled against his hold. He let go, but his body moved closer, not farther away, the rustle of his traditional robes the only sound besides their breathing in the quiet elevator.

With shock she realized there was no subtle sound of pulleys because he'd pushed the stop button.

She stared up at him, her heart in her throat. "Emir?"

"Sayed. My name is Sayed."

And she wasn't about to use it. Only she did, whispering, *"Sayed,"* in an involuntary expulsion of soft sound.

Satisfaction flared in his dark eyes, a line of color burnishing his cheekbones. For whatever reason, the emir liked hearing his name on her lips.

He touched the name badge attached to her black suit jacket. "Amari is not your name."

"It is." Her voice came out husky, her throat too tight for normal speech.

"Not your given name."

"Aaliyah," she offered before her self-protection kicked in.

"Lovely." He brushed the name tag again and, though it was solid plastic, she felt the touch as if it had been over bare skin. "Your parents are traditionalists."

"Not exactly." Liyah didn't consider Hena's decision to make an independent life for herself and her illegitimate daughter *traditional*.

Hena had simply wanted to give Liyah as many connections to the country of her mother's birth as she could. Hena had also said she'd wanted to speak hope for her daughter's life every time she used her name, which meant *high exalted one*.

It was another example of the deceased woman's more romantic nature than that of her pragmatic daughter.

Liyah doubted very much if Gene Chatsfield had anything to do with naming her at all.

"Your accent is American," Sayed observed.

"So is yours."

He shrugged. "I was educated in America from the age of thirteen. I did not return to Zeena Sahra to live until I finished graduate school."

She knew that. His older brother's tragic death in a bomb meant for the melech had changed the course of Sayed's life and his country's future.

Further political unrest in surrounding countries and concerns for their only remaining son's safety had pushed the melech and his queen to send Sayed to boarding school. It wasn't exactly a state secret.

Nor was the fact that Sayed had opted to continue his education through a bachelor's in world politics and a master's in management, but having him offer the information made something strange flutter in Liyah's belly.

Or maybe that was just his nearness.

The guest elevators at the Chatsfield were spacious by any definition, but the confined area *felt* small to Liyah.

"You're not very western in your outlook," she said, trying to ignore the unfamiliar desires and emotions roiling through her.

"I am the heart of Zeena Sahra. Should my people and their ways not be the center of mine?"

She didn't like how much his answer touched her. To cover her reaction she waved her hand between the two of them and said, "This isn't the way of Zeena Sahra."

"You are so sure?" he asked.

"Yes."

"So you have studied my country." He sounded way too happy about that possibility.

"Don't take it personally."

He laughed, the honest sound of genuine amusement more compelling than even the uninterrupted regard of the extremely handsome man. "You are not like other women."

"You're the emir."

"You are saying other women are awed by me."

She gave him a wry look and said dryly, "You're not conceited at all, are you?"

"Is it conceit to recognize the truth?"

She shook her head. Even arrogant, she found

this man irresistible and had the terrible suspicion he knew it, too.

Unsure how she got there, she felt the wall of the elevator at her back. Sayed's body was so close his outer robes brushed her. Her breath came out on a shocked gasp.

He brushed her lower lip with his fingertip. "Your mouth is luscious."

"This is a bad idea."

"Is it?" he asked, his head dipping toward hers.

"Yes." Was this how it had begun with her mother and father? "I'm not part of amenities."

No wonder Hena had spent so much effort warning Liyah against the seductions of men.

"I know." His tone rang with sincerity.

"I don't do elevator sex romps," she clarified, just in case he didn't get it.

Something flared in his dark gaze and Sayed stepped back, shaking his head. "I apologize, Miss Amari. I do not know what came over me."

"I'm sure you're used to women falling all over you," she offered by way of an explanation.

He frowned. "Is that meant to be a sop to my ego or a slam against it?"

"Neither?"

He shook his head again, as if trying to clear it.

She wondered if it worked. She would be grateful for a technique that brought back her own usual way of thinking, unobscured by this unwelcome and unfamiliar desire.

She did not know what else he might have said or how she would have responded because the telephone inside the elevator car rang. She opened the panel the handset resided behind and answered it.

"Amari here."

"Is the sheikh with you?" an unfamiliar voice demanded, and she wondered if Christos Giatrakos, the new CEO himself, had been called to deal with the highly unusual situation.

A shiver of apprehension skittered down her spine, until she realized that the tones had that quality that implied a certain age.

"Yes, the emir is here," she forced out, realizing in kind of a shocked daze that she might well be speaking to her father for the first time.

"Put him on."

"Yes, sir."

She reached toward Sayed with the phone, the cord not quite long enough. "Mr. Chatsfield would like to speak with you."

Sayed came closer and took the handset, careful not to touch her in the process.

She retreated to the other side of the elevator where she was forced to witness the one-sided conversation. Very little was actually said beyond the fact there was no problem and they would be arriving at the lobby level in a moment.

Even with her tendency to shut down, Liyah would have felt the need to explain herself, not so the emir of Zeena Sahra. If she had not witnessed his moment of shocked self-realization, she wouldn't believe he was discomfited in the least by their situation.

True to his word, the elevator doors were opening on the lobby level seconds later. Both the emir's personal bodyguard and Liyah's father were waiting on their arrival.

The conspicuous absence of anyone else to witness their exit from the elevator said more than words would have what everyone thought had been happening in the stopped elevator.

Offended by assumptions about her character so far from reality, Liyah walked out with her head high, her expression giving nothing of her inner turmoil away.

Making no effort to set her boss's mind at rest in regard to Liyah's behavior, the emir barely acknowledged Gene Chatsfield before waving his bodyguard onto the elevator with an imperious "Come, Yusuf."

"In my office," her father said in frigid tones as the elevator doors swished to a close.

The following ten minutes were some of the most uncomfortable of Liyah's life. Bad enough to be dressed down by the owner of the Chatsfield chain, but knowing the man was her father, as well, had intensified Liyah's humiliation at the encounter.

The short duration of her time in the elevator with the sheikh and her obvious lack of being mussed had saved her from an even worse lecture. However, Liyah had been left in no doubt that she was never to ignore hotel policy of employees vacating the main elevators when guests entered again.

Definitely *not* the moment in which to make herself known to Gene Chatsfield as the daughter he'd never met.

Sayed woke from a very vivid dream, his sex engorged and his heart beating rapidly.

It was not surprising the dream had not been about his fiancée. He had known Tahira, the daughter of a neighboring sheikh, since their betrothal when she was a mere infant. He had been thirteen and on the brink of leaving for boarding school in the States.

His feelings toward her had not changed appreciably since then.

The uncomfortable but also unsurprising reality was that the dream had centered on the beautiful Aaliyah Amari he'd met his first day in London. And thought about incessantly since.

He'd seen her in passing twice, once before the elevator incident and once since then. Both times his attention had been inexorably drawn to Aaliyah, but she'd done her best to pretend ignorance of his presence on the most recent occasion.

Understandably.

Nevertheless, even after the briefest collision with her emerald-green gaze, electric shocks had gone straight to his instant erection. And he'd almost stumbled.

Him.

Accused of being made of ice more than once, his disturbing reaction to this woman who had no place in his life bothered Sayed more than he wanted to admit. The elevator incident was still firmly in the realm of the inexplicable, no matter how much he'd tried to understand his own actions in the matter.

Sheikhs did not pant after chambermaids, not even those with additional responsibility. Aaliyah was of the servant class. He was an emir. He could not even consider an affair with her if he were so inclined.

Regardless, while Sayed had not been celibate for his entire adult life, he had been for the past three years.

Once Tahira had reached the age of majority and their betrothal had been announced officially, his honor demanded he cease sexual intimacy with other women. No one else seemed to expect it of him, but Sayed didn't live according to any viewpoint but his own.

However, his celibacy might well explain the intense and highly sexual dreams. Three years was a long time to go without for a thirty-six-year-old man who had been sexually active since his teens.

The knowledge that his sexual desert would end in a matter of weeks after he married Tahira gave him little comfort.

He could no more imagine taking the woman he still considered a girl, despite her twenty-four years, to bed than he could countenance giving in to his growing hunger for Aaliyah Amari.

CHAPTER THREE

LIYAH WATCHED HER father from the distance of the cavernous lobby.

If she wasn't sneaking in unnecessary glimpses of the emir, Liyah was straining for yet another impression of Gene Chatsfield. It was ridiculous.

Unable to deal with her attraction to Sayed in any other way than to avoid direct contact, she was no closer to coming to terms with the reality of her father, either.

And she felt like a coward.

Hena Amari had always been vocal in her praise of what she considered her daughter's intrepid and determined nature. Neither of which were at the forefront of Liyah's actions right now.

She needed to get her first meeting with Gene Chatsfield over with. If for no other reason than to tell him of her mother's death.

She sincerely doubted anyone else had done so. It wasn't something that human resources would have mentioned to the owner of the entire hotel chain.

The Chatsfield San Francisco had sent a beautiful bouquet of purple irises to the funeral; however, these were probably organized by Stephanie Carter and that was no indication their proprietor knew of his chambermaid's death.

Liyah watched as Gene stepped onto the elevator, no doubt headed to the penthouse-level suite he always occupied when he was in London.

The empty suite. Because his fiancée was out shopping and not expected back until after teatime.

Now would be the perfect time for Liyah to make herself known to him. Things with the hotel were running smoothly; there had been no further complications with the sheikh's visit.

And what was Liyah doing here if it wasn't to fulfill her mother's final request?

Unlike her half sister Lucilla Chatsfield, Liyah didn't want to make her career at the family hotel and certainly not simply to please her father. He hadn't exactly been supportive of Lucilla's career, his one child who had made it clear she was not only interested in the welfare of the hotels, but worked hard for the Chatsfield. Instead, her father had hired a man with a ruthless reputation and, if the rumors were true, Giatrakos was extending his own personal brand of punishment not only to Lucilla, but to the remaining Chatsfield siblings. The man was a dinosaur when it came to workplace ideals.

Besides, Liyah had no fantasies that Gene Chatsfield would publicly acknowledge *her*. Not after a lifetime of him not doing so.

Theirs would always have to be a private relationship. The Chatsfield name had spent enough time in the tabloids. Gene would never willingly be party to dragging it through the red ink of more media scrutiny.

But that didn't mean he wasn't interested in meeting his twenty-six-year-old daughter.

His payment of support, as modest as it had been, all the way through her college years indicated he felt something toward Liyah. If only obligation.

Just like her obligation to Hena's memory.

Right. It was time.

Taking a breath to calm her suddenly racing heartbeat, Liyah untucked her mother's locket from beneath her blouse. She'd worn it every day since Hena had given it to Liyah on her deathbed.

Curling her fingers around the metal warmed by her skin, Liyah took courage from the love and memories that it would always evoke and keyed the elevator for the penthouse level.

A few minutes later, Gene Chatsfield opened his suite's door, holding a mobile phone against his chest and wearing a puzzled expression on his features. "Yes, Amari?"

Something cold slithered down her spine at her father's use of her last name. But what else was he supposed to call her? He probably didn't even know her first name.

That would change in the next hour.

Dismissing the inevitable nerves, Liyah schooled her features into her most comfortable mask of unruffled dignity. "Mr. Chatsfield, I would appreciate a few moments of your time."

"If this is about your employment here, I have to tell you I trust my human resource and senior housekeeping staff implicitly. It's no use you looking for special favors from the proprietor and, quite frankly, in very poor taste."

"It's nothing like that. Please, Mr. Chatsfield."

For a moment, Gene Chatsfield looked torn. "Come in," he said, "and sit down. I just need two minutes." After the briefest of gestures to the sofa in the lounge area, Gene hovered in the doorway to the room beyond.

"I'm sick of it, Lucca."

Faintly embarrassed and very uncomfortable to be present for such a clearly personal conversation between Gene and his son, Liyah looked around the room. Beside a large, comfortable chair was a side table that held a glass of what looked like whiskey and a newspaper. The head-

line screamed across the room. Lucca Chatsfield
Does It Again!

What might have once been the amusing an-
tics of a world-renowned playboy—a stranger
to her—it now sickened her to know that these
scandalous exploits were from her own flesh
and blood. She had unfollowed @LuccaChats-
field, wanting no more distractions or information about her family.

"Just keep it off the internet, and for all our
sakes, stay the hell away from Twitter," Gene
growled into the phone before cutting the call
dead and turning his attention back to Liyah.

If anything, his frown turned more severe,
clearly ready to tackle what he saw as another
problem. "While I'm aware I must have a certain
reputation among the chambermaids, my days of
dallying in that direction are years in the past."

Liyah couldn't hide the revulsion even the
thought of what he was implying caused. "That
is *not* why I'm here."

Inexplicably, he smiled. "I'm glad to hear it.
My fiancée is a possessive woman."

And he was a former lothario with a past he
no doubt wanted to keep exactly where it was.
Buried.

"You know, this was a bad idea. I'm sorry I
bothered you." She couldn't promise it wouldn't

happen again, but she was leaning toward the idea that maybe…really, *it wouldn't.*

No matter what Hena had wanted.

"Nonsense. You've interrupted my afternoon for a reason. Come in." He stepped back and indicated with an imperious wave of his hand that she should enter.

"Are you sure you're not the emir around here?" she muttered under her breath as she did as he bid.

Apparently, he heard her, because he laughed, the sound startled. "You are no shrinking violet, I'll give you that, Amari."

"My name is Aaliyah, though I usually go by Liyah." It sounded more American, even if the spelling was pure Middle Eastern.

"We are not on a first-name basis," he replied with a return to his superior, if wary, demeanor of earlier.

She nodded acknowledgment even if she couldn't give verbal agreement. He was her father; they *should* be on a first-name basis.

He led her into a posh living room with cream furniture, the walls the same saffron as a great deal of the hotel. Recessed lighting glowed down from the arched ceiling and a fire burned in the ornate white marble fireplace.

"Please, sit down." He indicated one of the

armchairs near the fire before taking the one opposite.

She settled into the chair, her hands fisting against her skirt-covered thighs nervously. "I'm not sure how to start."

"The beginning is usually the best place."

She nodded and then had a thought. Taking the locket from around her throat she handed it to him.

"This is a lovely, antique piece of jewelry. Are you hoping to sell it?" he asked, sounding confused rather than offended by that prospect.

"No. Please open it and look at the pictures inside." One was of Liyah on her sixteenth birthday and the other was of Hena Amari at the same age.

She wouldn't have looked appreciably different at eighteen, the age she was when she had her short affair with Gene Chatsfield.

He looked at the pictures, his puzzled brow not smoothing. "You were a lovely girl and your sister, as well, but I'm not sure what else I'm looking at."

"The other woman isn't my sister. She was my mother."

He looked up then. "She's dead?"

Liyah nodded, holding back emotion that was still too raw.

"I am very sorry to hear that."

"Thank you. She didn't tell me about you until just before she died."

He frowned, his expression growing less confused and more cautious. "Perhaps you should tell me who *she* is and why she would presumably have told you about me."

"You don't recognize her?" Even after having time to really look at the picture?

It was small, but the likeness was a good one.

"No."

"That's…" She wanted to say *obscene,* but stopped herself. "Disappointing."

"I imagine, if you are here for the reason I believe you are."

"You know why I'm here?" she asked, a tiny bud of relief trying to unfurl inside her.

"It's not the first time this has happened."

"What exactly?"

"You're about to claim I am your father, are you not?"

"That happens to you a lot?" she demanded, both shocked and appalled. "How many innocent chambermaids did you seduce?"

"That is none of your business."

No, really, it wasn't.

Eyes narrowed, Liyah nevertheless nodded. "While I find it deplorable you apparently never even bothered to find out my first name from Mom, don't try pretending you didn't know of my existence. She told me about the support payments."

"Your mother's name?" he demanded in a voice icier than *she'd* ever managed.

"Hena Amari." There, that should at least clarify things. Though how he hadn't already made the connection with her last name, Liyah couldn't figure out.

"And I supposedly had a fruitful tryst with this Hena Amari. Did she work for one of my hotels, too? She must have, I kept my extramarital activities close to home in those days."

"She was your chambermaid at the Chatsfield San Francisco."

"What year?" he demanded.

She told him.

He shook his head. "While I am not proud of my behavior during that time in my life, neither am I going to roll over for blackmail."

"I'm not trying to blackmail you!"

"You mentioned support payments."

"That you made until I graduated from university. They weren't large, but they were consistent."

"Ah, so now we are getting somewhere."

"We are?" Liyah was more confused than her father had seemed when she first arrived.

"You're looking for money."

"I am not."

"Then why mention the support payments?"

"Because they're proof you knew about me," she said slowly and succinctly, as if speaking to a small child.

Either he was being deliberately obtuse, or something here was not as she believed it to be. The prospect of that truth made Liyah pull the familiar cold dignity around her more tightly.

"I never made any such payments."

"What? No, that's not possible." Liyah shook her head decisively. He was lying. He had to be. "Mom told me you weren't a bad man, just a man in a bad situation."

Hena had refused to name Liyah's father while living, but she'd done her best to give her daughter a positive impression of the absentee parent.

As positive as she could in the face of undeniable facts. The man had been much older and married. Hena had been a complete innocent, in America for the first time and too-easy prey.

"She said the support proved you cared about me even if you couldn't be in my life." Though that had been his choice, hadn't it?

He'd kept his affairs secret; he could have kept a minimal relationship with his illegitimate daughter just as heavily under wraps.

"It sounds to me like your mother said a great deal, much of it fabricated." He sounded

unimpressed and too matter-of-fact to be pre-
varicating.

Sick realization washed over Liyah in a cold,
unstoppable wave that made her feel like she was
drowning. She was breathing, but couldn't get
enough air. Betrayal choked her.

Her mother had lied to her.

The one person in her life Liyah had always
trusted. Her only family that mattered.

Something inside Liyah shattered, loosening
feelings and entrenched beliefs like flotsam in
the miasma of her emotional storm.

Liyah's entire reasoning behind following
through on Hena's last wish was false. Her father didn't know about Liyah, wanted nothing to
do with her and never would.

"I can only repeat, I never made any such
payments." There was no compassion, no understanding, in his cold blue eyes. "If you really
were my child and I had elected to help support
raising you, you can rest assured the monetary
stipend would not have been negligible."

She stood, her legs shaky—though she wasn't
about to let him know it—her heart a rock in her
chest. "I'm sorry I bothered you. I won't do so
again."

"See that you don't. Your regret would far
outweigh anything you might hope to gain." He
rose, as well, towering over her, despite the slight

stooping of age. "If you attempt to cash in on our supposed connection in *any way*, I won't hesitate to prosecute you to the fullest extent of the law."

She reeled back, feeling as if he'd struck her. "My mother was wrong."

"She certainly was to send you on this wild errand. Is she even dead? I doubt it?"

"Yes, the only parent that will *ever* matter to me died four months ago."

"And it took you this long to come find your supposed father? More like you worked out how to cash in on some convenient coincidences."

Drawing on the brittle exterior she'd had to show to the world too much in her life, Liyah lifted her head and looked at Gene Chatsfield like the worm he was. "The only convenience is the fact your hotel paid for my trip here."

"I will expect you to put in your notice tomorrow. I won't have a would-be blackmailer working in my hotel."

"I would leave right now but unlike some of the children *you* raised, I have a work ethic." With that, Liyah swept from the suite on legs that barely held her up.

Not that she'd let the man in the suite see her weakness. He'd gotten the single moment of vulnerability from her she would ever give him. The moment when she'd asked him in so many words to be her father.

She was on the elevator before Liyah remembered she'd left her mother's locket with Mr. Chatsfield. Only, when the elevator doors opened to the lobby, she found herself incapable of keying in access to the hotelier's floor again.

She stood there in a fugue of inner turmoil as two men got on the elevator with her. Liyah should have stepped off, not ridden it with guests.

She did nothing, turned away from them as one keyed access to the presidential level.

Realizing there was no way she was returning to the suite, she managed to press the button for her concierge level, not at all sure what she was going to do when she arrived there.

She only knew one thing with certainty. Liyah wasn't asking Gene Chatsfield for the necklace. She wasn't ever going to ask that man for anything again.

He'd most likely see she got it back via employee channels, anyway. And if he didn't?

Liyah would let go of the memento the same way she'd had to let go of her belief Hena Amari would never lie to her.

Her entire childhood had been influenced by the deception that her father knew and cared about her in even some minimal way. The realization he did not shouldn't be so devastating, but shards of pain splintered through Liyah's heart.

Only then did she realize how much it had

meant to her to believe she *had* a father, no matter how distant and anonymous.

Liyah tried to tell herself that her life was no different today than it had been yesterday. Gene Chatsfield had never been anything more than an ephemeral dream.

So, he denied his paternity? It didn't matter.

She wanted to believe that, but she'd never been good at lying to herself no matter how impenetrable the facade she offered the rest of the world.

Cold continued to seep through her, making her shiver as if she was standing at the bus stop in the winter's chill. Her usually quick brain was muzzy, her hands clammy, her heart beating a strange tattoo.

If she didn't know better, Liyah would think she was in shock.

Sounds came as if through a tunnel and colors were strangely sharp while actual details grew indistinct.

She felt like if she reached out to touch the wall, her hand would go right through it. Nothing felt real in the face of a lifetime and what amounted to a deathbed confession marred by lies.

Deceptions perpetrated by the one person she would never have looked for it from destroyed

Liyah's sense of reality, Gene Chatsfield's denial a blow she would have never expected it to be.

Despite her inner turmoil, clipped tones managed to draw Liyah's attention. Perhaps because they came from the one man who managed to occupy her thoughts more than her biological father.

Sayed spoke in Arabic to his personal bodyguard, the man she'd heard called Yusuf.

So furious he seemed unaware of Liyah's presence, she realized why as the import of his conversation hit her.

Apparently, Liyah wasn't alone in facing betrayal today. Unbelievably, the future emira of Zeena Sahra had eloped with a palace aid.

Another kind of shock echoed through Liyah. What woman would walk away from a lifetime with Sayed?

The doors whooshed open and she stepped onto the floor that had been blocked off for the harem of Sayed's entourage, one thought paramount. The no-longer-future emira's rooms would not be occupied. Not tomorrow, or any day thereafter for the next week.

Liyah's overwhelming need to be completely away from the potential of prying eyes had an outlet.

She kept her eye out for anyone in the hall, but it was blessedly empty. As much as she liked

Abdullah-Hasiba, Liyah felt an almost manic fear of being forced to speak with the older woman, or anyone else related to Sayed.

She was barely handling her own destructive revelations; Liyah wasn't up to hashing out the prince's woes with his loyal staff.

Using her pass card, she quietly let herself into the former fiancée's room. Tears Liyah never allowed herself to shed in front of her mother for Hena's sake, much less before strangers, were burning her throat and threatening to spill over.

Once inside the lavishly appointed suite, Liyah had no interest in the mint-green walls and elegant white accents and furniture. Her focus was entirely on the fully stocked liquor cabinet in the alcove between the suite's sitting room and small dining area.

The request for the full accompaniment of alcohol had surprised Liyah, but it had come from Tahira herself, rather than through Sayed's staff.

It was Liyah's job to see that hotel guest's requests were attended to, not determine their appropriateness.

Though considering the fact Sayed's suite had no alcohol and neither was any requested for his support staff, Liyah had thought it wasn't a habit he was aware his future emira indulged in.

It was pretty obvious in the face of recent

events that drinking wasn't the only thing Tahira had been hiding from her fiancé.

Liyah was on her third glass of smooth aged Scotch, without the dilution of ice, when she heard the telltale snick of a key card in the suite's door lock.

She watched with the fascination of a rabbit facing off a snake as the heavy wooden door swung inward.

The handsome but set face of Sheikh Sayed bin Falah al Zeena showed itself, along with his imposing six-foot-two-inch body clad in his usual designer suit under the traditional black men's *abaya*.

Dark eyes narrowed in shocked recognition.

CHAPTER FOUR

SAYED KNEW EXACTLY what drove him to his former fiancée's suite and it wasn't any form of sentimentality.

It was for the fully stocked liquor cabinet he could indulge in without witnesses.

He'd stopped in shock at the sight that greeted his eyes once inside, his body's instant response not as unwelcome as it would have been only two hours before.

Aaliyah Amari lounged on the sofa, a crystal glass in her hand, her emerald eyes widened in surprised befuddlement. The scent of a very good malt whiskey lingering in the air implied she'd come to Tahira's room for the same reason he had.

To drink.

On any other day, he would have been livid, demanding an explanation for her wholly unacceptable behavior. But today all his fury was used up in response to the betrayal dealt him by his betrothed.

"She's not here," Aaliyah said, her words drawled out carefully.

"I am aware."

Aaliyah blinked at him owlishly. "You're probably wondering why *I* am."

"It would appear you needed a drink and a private place to have it."

Her expression went slack. "How did you know?"

He shrugged.

"Have you been speaking to my father?" She leaned forward, her expression turning nothing short of surly.

The woman had to be inebriated already if she thought the emir of Zeena Sahra had taken it upon himself to converse with her parent. "If I have seen Mr. Amari, I am unaware of that fact."

Her lush lips parted, but the only sound that came out was a cross between a sigh and a hiccup.

He almost laughed. "You are drunk."

"I don't think so." Her lovely arched brows drew together in an adorable expression of thought. "I've only had three glasses. Is that enough to get drunk?"

"You've had three glasses?" he asked, shocked anew.

"Not full. I know how to pour a drink, even if I don't usually imbibe. I only poured to here." She indicated a level that would be the equivalent to a double.

"You've had six shots of whiskey."

"Oh." She frowned. "Is that bad?"

"It depends."

"On?"

"Why you're drinking."

"I learned someone I thought would never lie to me had done it my whole life, that I believed things that were no more than a fairy tale."

That sounded all too familiar. "I am sorry to hear that."

It was her turn to shrug, but in doing so she nearly dropped her mostly empty glass. "She said my father wasn't a bad man."

"She?" he heard himself prompting.

"My mom."

"You didn't know your father?" His life had not been the easy endeavor so many assumed of a man born to royalty, but he'd had his father.

A good man, Falah al Zeena might be melech to his people, but for Sayed, the older man wasn't just his king. He was and had always been Sayed's loving father—papa to a small boy and his closest confidant now.

"Not until recently." Aaliyah's bow-shaped lips turned down. "I think Mom was wrong."

"He *is* a bad man?" Sayed asked, the surreal conversation seeming to fit with the unbelievable day he'd already had.

Aaliyah sighed, the sound somehow endearing. "Not really, but he's not very nice."

"I think many might say the same about me."

"Probably."

He laughed. "You are supposed to disagree. Do you not realize that?"

"Oh, why? I think's it's the truth. You're too arrogant and imperious to be considered *nice*."

"I am emir."

"Exactly."

"You do not think a ruler can be kind?"

"Kind isn't the same as nice and you're not ruler yet, are you?"

"As emir I have many ruling responsibilities." Which were supposed to increase tenfold when he became melech after his wedding to Tahira.

A wedding that wasn't going to take place now, not after she'd eloped with a man a year her junior and significant levels beneath her in status.

"Okay."

"Okay what?"

"I'm not sure." She looked at him like he was supposed to explain the conversation to her.

"You're smashed."

"And you want to be."

"You're guessing."

"My brain may be fuzzy, but it's still working."

"Yes?"

"You guessed I wanted a private place to drink because you do, too."

"That's succinct reasoning for a woman who probably couldn't walk a straight line."

"I'd prefer not to try walking at all right now, thanks." She waved a surprisingly elegant hand.

"I'll get my own drink, then."

She made a sound like a snort, putting a serious dent in any semblance to elegance. "You were expecting me to do it?"

"Naturally." He failed to see why that should cause her so much amusement.

But his response was met with tipsy laughter. "You really have the entitlement thing down, don't you?"

"Is it not your job to serve me?" He dropped ice in a glass and poured a shot's worth of ouzo over it.

"You wanted to make this official?"

"What? No, of course not." He found himself taking a seat beside her on the sofa rather than settling into one of the armchairs. "You will tell no one of this."

She rolled her eyes at him and shook her head. "What is it with rich, powerful men assuming I have to be told that? Believe it or not, I don't need anyone knowing I was caught getting sloshed in a guest's room."

The mental eye roll was as palpable as if she'd done it with her glittery green gaze.

"Tahira won't need it." Not the room and not the liquor she'd ordered for her rooms. The words came out more pragmatic than bitter, surprising him.

Sayed might be undeniably enraged at Tahira's lack of commitment to duty, her deceptions and her timing, but it was equally undeniable that he felt no emotional reaction to her elopement with another man.

"That worked out conveniently for both of us."

That was drunken logic for you. "I would not be here if she had kept her promises," he pointed out.

"She ran off with someone else, right?"

"The press already have the story?" he demanded.

Things were going to get ugly very quickly, but for the first time in his memory, Sayed could not make himself care right at that moment. He'd lost his brother and the rest of his own childhood to politics and the violence they spawned in angry men.

Sayed had spent the intervening years taking on every duty assigned him, dismissing his own hopes and dreams to take on the welfare of a nation. He'd put duty and honor above his own happiness time and again, doing his best to fill an older brother's shoes he'd never been meant to walk in.

He was tired. Angry. Done. Not forever, but for tonight he wasn't emir. He was a man, a newly freed man.

"I spent my entire life being what and who I was supposed to," he offered, not sure why, but feeling the most shocking certainty that his confidences *were* safe with this woman.

Aaliyah drained the last bit of amber liquid from her glass. "Yes?"

"It was not as if I was attracted to Tahira. Marriage to a woman who seemed more like a little sister than a future wife did not appeal."

"But you never tried to back out of it."

"Naturally not."

"And that makes you angry now that she's taken off for the freedom of a life of obscurity."

"Are you sure you've had three doubles? You're very lucid in some moments."

Aaliyah giggled and then hiccupped and then stared at him as if she couldn't quite believe either sound had come from her mouth.

He found himself smiling when, ten minutes ago, he would have said that would be impossible. Even his fury was banking in favor of the constant burn of desire Aaliyah sparked in him.

She smiled tipsily. "You're both better off."

"That is a very naive view of the situation."

"Maybe." Aaliyah shrugged. "I was born to an amazing woman who gave up everything she knew of life to keep me, not a queen."

"My mother is amazing," he said, feeling strangely affronted.

"I know. I read about her. Melecha Durrah is both a gracious and kind queen. Everyone says so."

"Not *nice?*" he teased.

"I would not know. I've never met her."

"She is," he assured. "More so than either her husband or son."

"Nice can be overrated."

"Why do you say that?"

"My mother was too nice. If she'd ever just let herself get angry at the people who hurt her, she would have had a better life."

"Perhaps she enjoyed the peace of forgiveness."

"Maybe." Aaliyah stood, swaying in place. "I think I'll have another."

He jumped up and guided her back to the sofa. "After some water, I think."

"I don't want water."

"Yes, you do, you just don't know it." He

wasn't sure *anything* would prevent a hangover at this point, but staying hydrated would help.

"You're awfully bossy."

"So I've been told."

"I'm sure you have."

He shook his head, filling two glasses with ice from the bar. He snagged a couple liter bottles of water as well as the ouzo before carrying it all back to the sofa.

He put everything on the coffee table before pouring them both a glass of water and topping off his ouzo.

"You weren't even finished with your first drink," she commented after taking an obedient sip of water.

"You're five shots up on me."

"And you intend to catch up?"

Why not? "Yes."

"How did you know Princess Tahira had alcohol in her rooms?"

"I know everything about the people I need to." With one glaring exception.

"Not *everything*."

"No, not everything." Clearly, he hadn't known about the palace aid. "It would have been politic of you not to point that out."

Aaliyah shrugged. "I'm a lead chambermaid, not a politician."

"You don't act like any maid I've ever encountered."

"Gotten to know many of them, have you?" she asked with a surprisingly bitter suspicion.

"No, actually. That is precisely what makes you so different."

Her ruffled feathers settled around her. "Well, I don't usually work housekeeping. I was assistant manager of desk reception in my previous job."

"Why are you working as a maid now?"

"They wanted my mother, but she died."

"Your mother is gone, as well?" he asked, pity touching his heart as it rarely did.

"Yes. She was from Zeena Sahra."

"Did you come to London to be with the rest of your family?" There was a small community of Zeena Sahrans residing in the British city.

"The Amaris don't recognize me."

"But that's impossible." Family was sacrosanct in Zeena Sahran culture.

"Mom refused to allow someone else in the family to adopt and raise me. The Amaris refuse to recognize a bastard."

He frowned, inexplicable anger coursing through him. "Do not use such language to describe yourself. It is not seemly."

"Neither was offering to pay me off if I'd change my last name."

"They did that?" It boggled his mind.

Aaliyah nodded, an expression of deep vulnerability coming over her features he was fairly certain she was not aware was there. "No matter what Mom hoped, they were never going to accept me into the family. She is buried in the family plot. I won't be."

"It is their loss."

"I keep telling myself that, but you know? Sometimes it's hard to believe."

"Believe it."

"They're not alone. I am and I don't like it." She covered her mouth and stared suspiciously at him, as if he'd drawn the admission out of her rather than her offering it unasked for.

"No one should be abandoned by their family."

She tried to put on an insouciant expression that fell far short, but he wouldn't tell her so. He found he enjoyed seeing what he was sure others did not.

The true Aaliyah Amari.

"It happens." She shrugged and this time her glass tipped enough to spill its nearly full contents down the front of Aaliyah's inexpensive black suit jacket.

She didn't even jump, just looked down at the water-soaked jacket. "Oops."

"You are all wet."

"I am." She cocked her head to one side as if

studying him and finally said, "You could offer to get a towel."

"Should I?"

Instead of answering, Aaliyah unbuttoned the front and started shrugging the black fabric off her shoulders.

"What are you doing?" he demanded, his body tightening in a familiar way.

"Don't worry, I'm wearing a blouse underneath, but if I don't get this off, that will be soaked, too."

Once she removed her jacket, Sayed couldn't hold back his gasp. She'd been too late. The white cotton was wet and clinging to the skin of her torso and the lace-covered curves of her breasts.

Aaliyah looked down and made a moue of distaste his mother would have been proud of, then she giggled. "Too late."

"My very thought."

"I guess I'd better take this off, too."

His conscience demanded he discourage her from that particular course of action, but he refused to listen, watching in lustful fascination as she removed her uniform tie and then the soggy blouse.

Her lacy bra was surprisingly revealing.

"You like pretty lingerie," he said with a blatant shock that would have indicated the ouzo had already hit his system to anyone who knew him.

Sayed was not blatant. He was subtle. Especially in delicate situations like this one.

Aaliyah nodded. "Why shouldn't I? I have to dress conservatively for the job, but that doesn't mean I can't be as feminine as I like underneath."

"Your uniform does not mask your womanliness."

"Are you sure?" she asked very seriously. "I always thought it did."

Very decisive, he shook his head. "No."

"This isn't very modest, is it?" she asked in that way that said her brain was catching up to her actions.

"It is all right," he heard himself say.

"You would say that. You're a man."

"I am." Despite what many thought, he was indeed a flesh-and-blood male.

"Well, I know what to do." She nodded with exaggerated movement.

Expecting her to put her damp jacket back on, he sat blinking in lust-ridden surprise as she lifted her hands to fiddle with her hair at the back of her head.

A moment later long, black, silky waves of hair cascaded down over her shoulders and breasts. She arranged it so the wavy strands created a black silk blanket over the tempting mounds of flesh of her breasts.

"There." She smiled with satisfaction, clearly proud of herself.

"You believe that is more modest?" he asked, his voice cracking on the last word in a way it had not done in more than twenty years.

She looked down, as if trying to figure out why he would ask. "It covers the important bits."

"It does." In a way guaranteed to send his libido into overdrive.

She poured herself another glass of water, managing to do so without spilling any of the liquid. Though it was a close thing.

Taking a sip, she gave him a look of expectation.

"What?" he asked.

"It's your turn."

"To spill on myself. I do not think so."

"You don't have to spill your drink, but you're supposed to take off your outer robe and stuff."

"I am?" Had he fallen through the rabbit hole and not realized it?

"It's only fair."

That made surprising sense.

He stood up, a little startled at how difficult that simple act had been. "It is called an *abaya*."

"I know."

He let it slide from his shoulders, laying it over the back of the sofa.

"The gold around the collar with burgundy embroidery means you're a big mucky-muck in Zeena Sahra," Aaliyah said sagely.

"Yes."

"So does your *egal*. I think you should take it off."

"Why?" He never removed his *keffiyah* and *egal* in front of strangers.

The head covering and triple-banded braided cord that bespoke his position as prince were as much a part of him as his close-cropped beard.

"I think you could do with a few hours of not being emir."

Aaliyah's words resonating through him, he stared at her. "I think you are right."

Isn't that what he'd decided himself not minutes ago?

She nodded, her hair shifting to reveal glimpses of honey-colored flesh he had a near-irresistible urge to taste. The reasons for resisting were melting away with other inhibitions that came with his place of state.

"My current thoughts are definitely not appropriate for an emir," he admitted.

"So, take it off."

"Removing my *egal* won't take away my role."

"We'll pretend it does."

The idea was very appealing. He gave in and pulled off both the head covering and *egal* holding it in place.

"Now the suit jacket," she instructed.

"Are you trying to get me naked?"

"I don't think so?"

"You don't sound very sure." And looked adorably confused by the idea.

CHAPTER FIVE

AALIYAH'S BROWS DREW together in thought. "You're supposed to be even with me."

"It doesn't work that way."

"Yes, it does." She nodded, her head only wobbling a little, her expression all too serious.

There was something flawed in her logic, but he couldn't identify what just then.

Besides, he liked the idea of stripping away another layer of the trappings that separated him from this woman. It was as satisfying as removing the *egal* and *keffiyeh,* letting go of his position for just a few hours in the privacy of the hotel suite.

Inexplicably, his fingers shook as he stripped out of his hand-tailored jacket, burgundy silk tie and gray pinstriped dress shirt.

Aaliyah didn't seem to notice, her eyes eating him up in a very flattering way. After the hours spent building his muscles while honing fighting skills passed down for generations in his family, he had no false modesty.

But the way she looked at him was not simply that of a woman attracted to his fit body; it was more intense than that.

She watched him with a powerful hunger more honest than any expression he'd seen on a lover's face.

She made a soft sound that went straight to his groin. "Your hair is too short to cover any skin."

"You do not sound bothered by that fact."

She shook her head.

"Perhaps you have noticed, but there is already hair on my chest," he pointed out.

Taking after his ancestors, it wasn't too plentiful, but enough he did not look like a boy.

"Yes." She audibly swallowed. "Your nipples are hard."

"I bet yours are, too." And lusciously tempting.

"They are," she breathed out.

He had to swallow a groan. "Drink more water. I'm having another ouzo." It tasted about a hundred proof and he rarely drank, but she wasn't outdoing him.

They both slammed their drinks back. Funnily enough, she choke-coughed on her water. His ouzo had gone down smooth as glass.

They sat in silent contemplation for long seconds.

"You wanted me," she said, her expression thoughtful. "That day in the elevator."

As if he needed reminding of when that might have been. He didn't because the desire had not left him since the first moment he'd seen Aaliyah.

"Yes," he said when it appeared she was waiting for him to reply in some way.

He still did. Intensely. Even painfully.

His sex was harder than any muscle in his body right now—and he had abs of rock that could withstand blow after blow from a sparring partner.

"I've never had sex in an elevator," she admitted like it was a deep, dark—even shameful—secret.

"I haven't, either."

"Oh."

"I am not certain it's as common an occurrence as romance movies would have us believe."

"You watch romantic comedies?" she asked.

He shrugged. "My mother enjoys them. My father and I usually defer to her when we have an opportunity to watch a movie as a family."

"That's sweet."

He was unaccustomed to being thought of as sweet and did not want to dwell on it. "Gene Chatsfield would have been very angry if there'd been evidence of sex that day, I believe."

"He was mad enough," she said dismissively.

"You don't sound too worried about that."

"I'm not." Her lovely features twisted in a scowl. "I'm leaving the Chatsfield."

He would have asked why, but Sayed's mouth went dry as she shifted to put her water glass down on the coffee table. Her hair fell away, exposing one breast. The dark nipple under champagne-colored lace as hard and delicious looking as he'd imagined it to be.

He cleared his throat and poured another glass of ouzo. "Three years is a very long time."

"Yes?" She blinked at him in more charming confusion.

"Yes." He tossed back the shot and put the glass down. "Without sex. It is a very long time."

"I wouldn't know."

"No?" She was sexually active? That was a good thing, considering the things he was thinking about doing.

"Nope." She hiccupped, covered her mouth and then laughed. "Sorry about that."

He shook his head, his focus on her seminudity, not her hiccups. "It is nothing."

"So, you're saying you've gone without sex for *three* years?" Her voice was laced with both disbelief and shock.

"I have." And considering Tahira's recent actions, he seriously doubted his ex-fiancée could say the same.

Aaliyah gave him a probing look. "Are you telling me the truth?"

"Why would I lie?" he asked with more genuine curiosity than offense, though he was unused to having his words questioned.

"Because you're hoping to talk me into bed?"

"I do not need to go for the sympathy vote to get a woman into my bed."

"No, you probably don't." She looked him over in a manner that was both innocent and lascivious.

He flexed his chest muscles for her and groaned when her beautiful green eyes grew dark and bottomless with desire as she inhaled sharply. "You probably have loads of women panting after you."

"I would not know. I spend very little time with single women these days." His own honor mocked him in ways he'd never share with another.

"Why?"

"I was a betrothed man."

"Oh." She smiled, appearing very happy with some thought she was having. "You really are one of those guys."

"What guys?"

"The ones who know how to be faithful, even before marriage."

"I am not perfect, but once Tahira came of age and our engagement was made official, it would have been wrong to continue having lovers."

"You never considered having sex with her... in *three* years? She never offered?"

"No."

"That's, um..."

"Proper."

Her full lips turned down in a frown. "Not what I was thinking."

"Pathetic?" Deluded of him? *Sad?*

He did not think that anything could cool his ardor, but the prospect that she pitied him proved extremely effective. He did not need pity sex, nor would his pride allow him to accept it, no matter how much he wanted her.

"I'm pretty sure *pathetic* is never a word anyone would use to describe you. I was going to say maybe you should have taken that as a warning."

Just like that, the craving was back, his sex pressing against the confinement of his trousers.

"Warning?" he asked, not understanding.

"Presumably, she was just as happy to remain celibate."

"At least with me, yes."

"So, neither of you were sexually attracted to each other?"

"It would appear not."

"You didn't think that was a problem?"

"Marriages among those in position are not made for the same reasons as in your world."

"Elitist much?"

He shrugged. He would not deny it. "Our worlds are barely in the same solar system."

"Wow. It's really true, *in vino veritas*. Although that's ouzo you're drinking, not wine."

"I assure you, I do not need spirits to tell the truth."

"Are you really that arrogant?"

"I'm not sure what you mean."

"Of course. Our worlds are too far apart for us to communicate." Her voice was laced with unmistakable sarcasm.

His wasn't when he said, "Right now, we're in the same space."

It was kind of amazing, really. That he would be alone in a place of privacy with this woman who was a maid, but whom he wanted more than he had any woman in his memory.

Her head tipped slightly and she looked up at him in unconscious sensuality. "We are, aren't we?"

"It is a moment out of time."

She laughed out loud. "Arrogant and cheesy. Why do I still want to kiss you?"

He did not understand what she found so

amusing. This was a moment that would never be repeated, could never be repeated. Yet he was grateful that destiny had written their meeting—here in this room that would never see his ex-betrothed—into their stars.

"Why shouldn't you want to kiss me?" he asked, certain he wanted it enough for both of them but aware that if she didn't he would do nothing about his own desires.

That damnable honor again.

"You think you are too good for me."

"No." He was shocked. "I did not say this."

"What about the whole different-worlds thing?" she asked, sounding hurt.

Which had never been his intention. "That is reality, not a judgment on either of our values as human beings. There are emirs in neighboring countries I would prefer never to have to interact with again."

"Really?"

"Absolutely."

"And me?"

"It would be my great delight to be able to spend more time with you," he said with more honesty than he ever offered.

"But?"

"But an emir cannot have even a temporary relationship with a hotel maid. Life is not a fairy tale." No matter how much he might wish otherwise.

"And you are certainly no Prince Charming."

The fact she apparently found him lacking bothered him, but he did not understand why it should. "No, I have never pretended to be anything but a man."

"Who is prince of his people."

"Exactly."

She looked at him strangely. "You really don't mean to be arrogant, do you?"

"No."

"You are, though. Just in case you ever wondered."

He found himself laughing. "Duly noted."

"You're not offended."

"Why should I be?"

"Because the opinion of a mere hotel maid doesn't matter, does it?"

"Of course your viewpoint is important." More important than he wanted to admit.

"You sound like a politician."

"I *am* a politician." Though not one that could be voted out of office.

Diplomacy was nevertheless very important in his life. He wasn't being diplomatic with her, however. He meant his words. For reasons he could not identify, her opinion mattered.

"You're very sexy for a politician." She sounded surprised by that fact.

Or perhaps it was her own admission of it.

Unable to bank the hunger any longer, he leaned forward. "I am glad you think so."

"You're going to kiss me," she whispered as his mouth was centimeters from hers.

He didn't bother to give a verbal reply, but pressed his mouth to hers. At first, she acted like she didn't know what to do, but then her lips softened and she let them mold to his.

And he understood her initial reticence. She'd said she didn't do one-night stands; naturally, she would have reservations about what was about to happen between them.

With great reluctance, he pulled his lips from hers. "We cannot have more than one night," he felt compelled to point out one last time.

He was still a man of honor, no matter how inconvenient.

Liyah had to process Sayed's words and what they meant before she could reply. "I know."

He'd made their short-term incompatibility perfectly clear. And she didn't care. She'd spent her entire life listening to her mother preach against easy familiarity with men.

Liyah had not dated in high school and only rarely in college, but she'd never allowed anything beyond simple kisses. She'd maintained her virtue on behalf of Hena Amari, to prove something that was forever denied her.

Her daughter's worthiness to be recognized by the Amari family.

She would never know that acceptance, but she *was* worthy to carry the Amari name. More worthy than those who would turn their back on Hena because her love for her child was too great to let Liyah go.

Liyah had remained chaste to prove to them all, but most especially Hena, that her mother had raised her better than any of them could have. Proving something to a woman who was irrevocably gone from Liyah's life, or people who simply did not matter, seemed beyond ridiculous.

Even to her alcohol-addled brain.

She had an entire life of being alone to look forward to. For this night, she would experience intimacy she'd always denied herself and might never know again.

No matter how melodramatic she told herself the sentiment was, Liyah had the distinct feeling no other man after this one would ever suffice.

Was love at first sight real, or was this just lust?

Liyah did not know, but the feelings she had for this arrogant sheikh went beyond anything she'd ever experienced.

She'd always thought her mother had been doing some kind of penance in never dating or seeking out another relationship, but maybe it was even simpler. Maybe Hena Amari had never stopped loving Gene Chatsfield.

And he hadn't even remembered what she looked like, much less her name.

Pushing those disturbing thoughts away, Liyah focused entirely on the man before her, the one whose kiss had touched her more deeply than she thought possible.

Sayed breathed against her lips, the soft puffs of air brushing them in a gentle caress. "I want to kiss you again."

She sighed softly. "I'd like that." A lot.

He didn't ask again, but put his desires into action, this time placing one hand behind her head. She found the control inherent in the action entirely in line with the man's nature.

What surprised her was how much she enjoyed it. She *liked* the way he helped her angle her head for the best connection, but she burned with the way his mouth felt against hers.

It was amazing and sent more sparks of unfamiliar need along her nerve endings. She wanted so much more than just a simple kiss. Not that this kiss felt simple. Decadent, delicious and completely addictive—his lips were lethal to her restraint.

One kiss melted into another until she realized what he wanted as his tongue slid along her lips pressing gently at the seam of her mouth. Liyah let him in and shuddered as the intimacy of their connection went to a whole new level.

He tasted like licorice and…*another person.* Liyah had never had a man's tongue slide along her own, had never experienced this level of familiarity with another person's mouth.

It was erotic in a way she never would have expected, making her want more. More of what, she wasn't sure.

But definitely more.

He cupped her breast and then she knew. She wanted more of *that.*

The thin layer of her bra might as well not even be there. Everywhere his hand had contact tingled, sending bursts of bliss arcing through her.

Warm masculine fingers caressed her, kneading her curve and brushing across her nipple. Her entire body went rigid at the electric jolts going directly from her aching peak to the core of her being.

Was this normal? Could ecstasy be this easy to achieve?

All the women's magazines made it sound a lot more complicated.

He gently pinched her nipple between his

thumb and forefinger, his tongue playing a mating dance with her mouth she'd never known but recognized nevertheless.

And she realized what she was feeling *wasn't* the ultimate in ecstasy. Because it kept building. One pleasure on top of another. Every sensation more intense than the last, her entire body heating as her blood rushed.

If this wasn't a climax, she wasn't entirely sure she was going to survive one.

But, oh, she was willing to try.

Sayed broke the kiss, the sound of their panting breaths loud to her ears. "Are you certain you want this?"

She nodded, unable to get a single word out.

"You understand, tomorrow I am again the emir of Zeena Sahra."

"But tonight you are just a man," she reminded him in a desire-laden whisper.

"Yes." The sound was closer to a growl than a word.

He kissed her again, this time his mouth devouring hers, his hold on her head implacably keeping her lips right where he wanted them. His aggressive passion might have frightened her but for the gentle way he continued to knead her breast and rasp her nipple.

Putting off a lifetime of restraint, she reached out to do some of her own sensual exploration.

His skin was hot against her fingertips and smoother than she expected. The black curls of hair on his chest were also surprisingly silky, his small male nipples ridged.

There was nothing soft about the layers of muscle bunching under her touch, though.

Chest, biceps and abdomen cut with defined muscles.

His body was so different than hers.

Sure, there was the male/female thing. But it was so much more than that.

Wearing the *egal,* or not, Sayed exuded power. He would always be alpha, never the beta. His physical and mental strength was awe-inspiring and in this moment those traits inspired her arousal, as well.

So focused on experiencing his body, she didn't notice his hands moving at first.

But when he unclipped her bra with a single efficient movement and peeled the lace-and-silky fabric away from her body, she couldn't ignore that.

Her already-hard peaks pebbled tighter at the direct exposure to air. She'd felt that hundreds of times in her life, when she undressed for bed.

What she'd *never* felt was the corresponding throb between her legs she experienced now. Or this new need to be touched *there*.

A desire she could only express with wordless whimpers and the tilting of her pelvis in a wanton display that should have mortified her.

It didn't.

His big hands slid around her sides and up her rib cage, leaving prickles of arousal in their wake until he cradled both her breasts.

"Lovely." Approval laced his tone. "A truly sweet handful."

"You have big hands. So hot," she rambled.

It was only when his rich laughter washed over her that Liyah realized how her words could be taken.

"I didn't mean to say I'm…that's not…"

He brushed his lips over hers. "Shh. You are perfect. We will leave it at that."

She had no chance to reply as his thumbs swiped over her electrified nipples. She'd thought the thin barrier of silk had made no difference in how these caresses felt, but she'd been wrong. Very, very wrong.

While the sensation of emptiness and need grew in her core, the rest of Liyah's body grew increasingly sensitive. Heat washing over in wave after wave of unadulterated lust, her skin ached for his touch in a way she hadn't even known was possible.

He seemed to understand, because his caresses moved on from her breasts to brush over her stomach, along her sides and right up to her underarms. Usually ticklish, the only response this unexpected touch elicited was gasping shivers and a hope he would not stop.

Inundated by sensations so intense she couldn't hope to distinguish one from the other, she moaned long and low.

His hands tightened into a hold on her waist, his fingers squeezing and releasing in quick succession. "You are so responsive."

"You make me *feel*." Liyah had spent her entire life hiding behind a buttoned-down facade which allowed for almost no emotion.

Feelings were dangerous.

But she'd found an inexplicable, if temporary, safety in this man's arms.

He kissed along the underside of her jaw, teasing her skin with the edge of his teeth and sending shivers cascading along her nerve endings. "You are far more intoxicating than the ouzo."

"You, too." She wished she could be more eloquent, but Liyah had no experience in this kind of talk and had no response but bare honesty.

He didn't seem to mind her lack of dramatic articulation as he intensified the sensual onslaught of his hands and mouth on her body.

CHAPTER SIX

SAYED PULLED BACK, giving her a probing look with his dark brown gaze. "You are not drunk."

It was a statement, but there was a question in the espresso eyes that demanded her undivided attention.

Even inebriated, Liyah realized that if she admitted to how inexperienced she was with alcohol, never mind sex, he would stop. The man had an overdeveloped sense of honor.

But regardless if she *was* a little tipsy, Liyah knew what she wanted. And it wasn't for him to stop.

"No." She turned her head, brushing his strong jaw with her lips, inhaling his spicy masculine scent. "If anyone is taking advantage, it's me."

There, she'd managed to sound both sober and in possession of her faculties. And honest. Because it was the truth. She'd never been *all that* and she knew it, but this amazing man wanted to make love with her.

No matter how much he'd claimed to want Liyah before, he wouldn't have acted on that desire without this particular unbelievable set of circumstances. He'd said it himself.

Their worlds didn't overlap. Not even a little.

"Then no one is taking advantage," he stated very firmly as his hands moved to the fastening on her skirt. "I believe it is time to remove more layers of the lives we choose not to acknowledge tonight."

"Yes." She didn't want any reminders of her job at the Chatsfield or why she'd taken it.

Shockingly, Liyah felt no hesitation about taking off the rest of her clothes. Especially as it appeared Sayed was intent on helping her.

Though she'd never been naked with a man before, wasn't accustomed to exposing her body to anyone for that matter. Hena had raised Liyah to be extremely modest, even among her female peers at school.

A lifetime's modesty melted under the heat of his desire and she did her best to help him undress, as well.

When they were both completely nude, no outward sign of their usual roles, he nodded with satisfaction. "Perfect."

"You are."

He smiled, the expression somehow rapacious. "Thank you."

"You're welcome." She was barely aware of what she was saying.

Her mind so preoccupied with the sight of acres of muscular bronzed flesh, she relied on rote response.

He moved toward her with the grace of a predator. "I hope you are ready for this."

She did, too.

He stopped in front of her. "I am breaking a three-year fast. Prepare yourself. I plan to feast on you."

Managing a bare nod, she shuddered at the words, but even more at his expression.

With practiced ease, he swung her up into his arms, the naked skin all along one side of her body pressed to his front.

She gasped.

"Couch sex is for when the comfort of a bed is not available." He swung them around and started walking to the suite's bedroom.

She didn't argue, just leaned forward and started placing tasting kisses against whatever skin she could reach.

Salt and unexpected sweetness burst over her taste buds.

The thought of making love for the first and only time with Sayed in the bed reserved for the woman he had intended to marry resonated with a strange sense of rightness.

While Liyah had no hope of ever being that woman, for tonight she was undeniably *his*.

He managed to pull back the covers and lay her on the bed without dropping her, or even unduly jostling her.

"You're pretty good at this," she said as he released her, impressed.

Sayed straightened, giving her full view of his amazing body, his expression confused in a way she was pretty sure it never was. "I'm sorry?"

"The whole getting-me-into-bed thing," she explained. "You were smoother than jazz."

"Smoother than jazz?" he asked with humor. "Really?"

She shrugged, unworried if her metaphor came off as campy. It's exactly what she meant. "No music is smoother."

"Perhaps I should be happy you didn't compare me to custard." He stood up.

She giggled and covered her mouth at the unfamiliar sound coming from her. "Maybe."

He shook his head, but his look was indulgent. He moved to join her on the bed.

"I suppose you have loads of experience carrying women to bed."

He stopped, sitting on the edge of the mattress, and looked down at her. "Actually, not so much." His dark gaze smoldered. "You are an exception in more than one way."

"The whole not-bedding-a-lowly-hotel-maid thing?" she teased, her confidence boosted by her certainty that was exactly what Sayed was about to do.

"Among other things."

"You're saying you don't usually carry your conquests to bed?"

"I cannot think of another instance."

At his admission, heat poured into places she wasn't used to feeling anything and she found it hard to continue their repartee. "For three years, anyway."

"Ever."

"Oh." That was…it was just…kind of amazing and more than she wanted to dwell on right now, if she wanted to keep her few working synapses continuing to connect in her brain. "I guess it's just instinct."

He laughed, the sound arresting and incredibly sexy.

Her chest felt tight. "Sayed…"

He cursed, his humor disappearing in an instant, replaced by that power-driven intensity she was so drawn to.

"What?" she asked, not sure what she'd done.

"Say it again."

"I don't know what you mean?"

He put his hands down and leaned forward,

pressing the pillow on either side of her head, his face only inches from hers. "My name."

His name? Her befuddled brain tried to make sense of his request. "Sheikh Say—"

"No," he said with quiet intensity. "Not my title. My *name*."

"Sayed." If the word held more emotion when she said it, she refused to acknowledge it.

Something flared in his espresso eyes and then his lips were on hers again. Though she'd been sure they'd reached the pinnacle of passionate kisses already, she realized quickly how wrong she'd been.

He shifted to lie beside her and pressed his body against hers, his hardness rubbing along her thigh. Another set of new and wonderful sensations beset her.

Liyah moved restlessly, her legs falling open.

He laid one hand between them, covering her feminine curls and most private flesh. "This is mine."

She had no thought to deny him. "Yes."

"Tonight is ours and you will be mine in every way."

Her answer was a wordless cry as he shifted and put his mouth over one of her nipples.

It was the most incredible feeling she'd ever known—the wet sucking heat, the sizzling jolts of pleasure shooting outward and through her body from that swollen bit of flesh, unbelievable.

Then his finger dipped into that most intimate place and she realized once again she'd been wrong. There was definitely more she could feel, more she could experience.

And more.

And more.

And more.

One sensation blended into another, her need for his touch growing in exponential proportion to every caress he gave her.

His fingers rolled slickly over a bundle of nerves even more potent than her nipples and she cried out. She knew about her clitoris. She hadn't grown up in a cave, but she had been raised to *never* talk about sexual things.

Not with her mother. Not with the other girls at school. Not with anyone. Sex was an entirely taboo subject with Hena Amari and she'd made sure Liyah saw it that way, too.

Liyah had spent her life excelling in school and then her career. She was almost as much a virgin in purely social interaction as sex. Sayed's intimate touch was the first time Liyah had ever realized exactly *where* that particular bundle of nerves was.

And he knew *how* to manipulate it for maximum impact, which he proved with expert caresses. Delight filled her, pushing from the inside outward, making her feel like her skin was too tight for her body.

It built and built, making her wonder how much more intense it could get as her sense of time and even her own person drowned in a pool of bliss.

Then something shattered inside her, the ecstasy exploding in shards of sharp rapture and she screamed. His name.

A long, pleasure-laden wail.

His mouth came off her nipple as he lifted his head, those magical fingers still moving in gentle circles as their gazes met. Satisfaction mixed with untamed hunger in his.

Barely touching her, he continued to cause tremors and contractions throughout her body. "You are so beautiful in your passion, *habibti.*"

His words and the endearment were as potent as his most intimate caress. Oh, she knew he didn't mean she really was his love, but Liyah's heart squeezed, anyway. He could have used *aashitii,* an endearment appropriate for an extramarital lover, but much less tender.

Tonight Liyah could be his *habibti.*

Tension still thrumming through her and unable to process the unfamiliar and overwhelming reactions of her body, Liyah's head rolled side to side on the pillow.

"Sayed." That was all she could say. Over and over again.

Despite imbibing copious amounts of alcohol and his easy use of *habibti,* Liyah did not have the courage to call him sweetheart, or lover, in English or Arabic.

And he *liked* when she said his name. So she did it again and again, her vocabulary shrunken to that single word.

He surged up over her, his big body settling between her legs. Sayed kissed her again, stealing his name right from her lips.

His rigid sex rubbed against her where his fingers had been, sending little shocks along her nerve endings, drawing forth a new kind of passion from her.

It wasn't just pleasure. It was the need to have him joined to her body in the most intimate way possible.

He broke the kiss, his breathing as heavy as hers. "We need a condom."

"A condom?" she asked, her mind hazy with drink and passion.

"Yes." He groaned. "You do not have one." He cursed, his body filling with a different kind of tension. "Of course you do not. This is not your room. You would not carry such a thing with you in your work uniform."

She was kind of impressed with how many

thoughts he managed to string together. The gist of them finally penetrated her own muzzy focus. They needed a condom and he didn't have one.

"Look in the drawer beside the bed."

He stared down at her, his stillness almost scary. "Did Tahira request them?"

"No." Liyah didn't even try to stifle the alien need to comfort, reaching up with an appeasing touch. "She was your fiancée. It seemed an expedient item to provide."

"Presumptuous."

Liyah just looked at him.

He moved to get what they needed, never quite losing contact with her body. Moments later, he settled back into his intimate position between her legs after putting on a condom from the brand-new box she'd put there herself in anticipation of an engaged couple's stay at the hotel.

His smile could have melted ice a lot thicker than that around Liyah's heart. "Perhaps *expedient* is the right word."

Her answering smile was as inevitable as what came next.

Sayed shifted so he pressed against the opening to her body. Everything inside Liyah stilled, her world shrunk down to this exact moment, this space, the breaths they shared between them. Nothing outside Sayed had a hope of registering.

Not with him on the brink of joining them

in the most intimate way, an experience that if Liyah was honest with herself she'd never actually expected to have. With anyone, much less this prince.

"This is going to be hard and fast." The words were guttural and low. "I am too excited."

Despite their detour into the mundane, she was still floating on a cloud of bliss, pretty sure fast and hard would work for her. "It's all right."

She wanted—no, *craved for*—him to experience the same pleasure she had.

He shook his head. "You are too perfect, *habibti.*"

"Not per—" Her words choked off abruptly as he pressed for entry.

Even though he'd warned her he was going to go fast, he moved inside her body with measured deliberation.

Liyah stretched around him, feeling full and connected like she'd never been to another person. Then a sharp sting shot through her core, making her gasp.

He must have encountered the barrier to her body. Liyah didn't feel like she was tearing, more like a stabbing pain.

He looked down at her. "It is good?"

She doubted he realized he'd asked the question in Arabic.

"Yes." It *was* good, even if it hurt.

"You are so tight."

She could only nod, gritting her teeth against the searing ache.

He drew back a little.

Despite the pain, she whimpered in protest at his withdrawal. "No."

His own breathing labored, his jaw was clenched as tight as hers, his arms shaking. And she realized it was using all his control to hold back.

Unfamiliar emotion seeped past the barrier around Liyah's heart.

"I'm not going anywhere, *ya ghazal*." He laughed, the sound sexy and dark. "Believe it."

Again, his endearment touched her more deeply than he probably meant it to, but Liyah's mother used to call her a gazelle. She'd claimed Liyah had the gracefulness and beauty of the animal so often used in Arabic poetry.

Sayed's addition of the possessive *my* only added to its impact, insuring this experience went far beyond the physical for Liyah.

He pressed forward again, the pain so sharp she couldn't breathe. She bit back a cry, terrified he would stop. And was infinitely grateful she had when the pain transformed into a whole new level of pleasure.

"That is it," he gritted out. "You have relaxed."

"More than," she managed to gasp out.

"You said you had not been on a sexual fast."

She just shook her head.

"Say what you like, *habibti,* but no woman is this tight and tense upon initial penetration when she has been sexually active regularly."

"I want you."

"I have no doubts." He thrust once, twice, three times.

Her body reacted with delight even as residual pain hung at the edges of pleasure.

"I admit I like knowing I am the first in a while."

She swallowed, trying to agree, unable to get another word out as he continued his slow, sure thrusts.

"Tonight, you are absolutely mine," he claimed a second time with an almost savage satisfaction.

And once again, she could only nod, the overwhelming ecstasy of the moment crashing over her.

For tonight, she wasn't just his.

He was hers.

Inside and surrounding her with his big body.

"Ready?" he asked her.

"Yes," she finally managed. Though she had no idea what she was supposed to be ready for.

Weren't they already making love?

He pulled back and then surged forward powerfully.

Oh. Yes.

All vestiges of pain drowned in ecstasy as he pistoned inside her body again and again. Here was the speed and intensity he'd warned her about.

Her body tightened under and around him as indescribable pleasure built again.

Her climax took her by surprise, the waves of bliss so intense she couldn't even cry out this time, her throat strained with a silent scream.

Moments later, Sayed went rigid above her, his shout ringing in the room around them.

And her pleasure was complete.

He collapsed down, but somehow managed to keep most of his weight from crushing her. "I am sorry, *ya ghazal*."

"Why?"

"That was too fast."

"But it felt incredible." A sudden thought worried her, and because her inhibitions were down, it came right out of her mouth. "Didn't you think so?"

"Oh, yes, *habibti*. But if I had lasted longer, it would have been mind-blowing."

He was still hard inside her.

She smiled up at him. "Show me."

He did.

Sayed woke to the pleasure of a warm, silken body against him. He opened his eyes cautiously, the early-morning sun revealing not his suite but another luxurious room.

Tahira's suite.

Tahira. Memories came crashing back. She'd eloped with a palace aid. And he'd come here to drown his sorrows in ouzo, only to end up experiencing the most intense and pleasurable night of his life.

Thankful he did not get hangovers, he tipped his head to see the top of Aaliyah's dark head peaking above the sheet. She was curled on her side, the Egyptian cotton sheet pulled up to cover her face, even as her body snuggled trustingly into his.

Which shocked him.

She might be used to sleeping with someone else, but he was not.

Sayed never took lovers to his own bed and had never spent the night in theirs.

Yet he'd slept more soundly last night than he had in months, even with the knowledge of Tahira's betrayal and its ramifications looming over him.

It must have been the ouzo.

He started to tug his hand back from where it rested against Aaliyah's stomach and she made a soft sound in her sleep, showing no signs of waking. For some reason he was loath to relinquish contact with her soft skin and he allowed his hand to settle again.

Just for a moment.

He could not make himself regret giving in to his desire for the beautiful Aaliyah Amari.

Nor could he allow himself to service the craving she elicited in him again.

Even if he could remain for the additional week in London he had planned, it would be a bad idea.

Regardless, he had to return to Zeena Sahra immediately.

The lack of a wedding between him and Tahira would have far-reaching political ramifications. Not least of which was the fact no emir had progressed to melech of Zeena Sahra while still a bachelor in the entire history of his country.

He and his father would have to find another suitable matrimonial prospect for Sayed, and very quickly, if they wished to minimize their international embarrassment.

His father.

Damn it.

Sayed should have called the older man the night before. He would have to do so very soon.

Should he wake Aaliyah before he left? It might be more comfortable for both of them to avoid the morning after.

However, it was inevitable, he realized.

Sayed wasn't about to do the walk of shame down the corridors of the hotel back to his suite in yesterday's no doubt hopelessly wrinkled suit.

With reluctance he could not deny but nevertheless had to ignore, Sayed removed the arm he had curled loosely around Aaliyah. She mumbled and stretched one leg so it brushed his provocatively but, once again, did not wake.

With more effort than it should have taken to make himself do it, Sayed moved so he was sitting on the side of the bed and reached for the phone.

Calling Yusuf, he instructed his personal bodyguard to bring him fresh clothing.

"Your parents both called yesterday."

"You handled it with tact and aplomb as usual, I am sure, Yusuf." The man was Sayed's personal bodyguard, not assistant, but he handled things too sensitive for Duwad or Abdullah-Hasiba.

Yusuf was the only person who had known where Sayed had ended up the night before. In fact, the bodyguard had suggested it.

"I did."

"Good."

Aaliyah groaned, moving beside him.

"You are not alone, Emir?" Yusuf asked.

"No."

"Do you need me to take care of it?"

The idea of his old friend *handling* Aaliyah as

he had others of Sayed's bed partners in the past was not acceptable. "No."

"She needs to sign a nondisclosure agreement."

"She won't say anything, Yusuf. She's not that type of woman." Sayed knew how hopelessly naive he sounded and he hadn't been that innocently trusting since his brother's assassination all those years ago.

Still, he was certain he was right.

"Keep her there until I arrive," Yusuf instructed.

"Did you forget who is emir here?"

Aaliyah's head came up from under the sheet at that and she stared at him with wide eyes.

"I never forget my duty to you, O' Emir." Sarcasm dripped from Yusuf's tone.

"It is not your duty I'm questioning." Just the other man's willingness to follow a direct order.

Not something either of them had high expectations of after all their years of friendship.

"Think with your big head here, Sayed," Yusuf almost pleaded. "If she is not there when I arrive, I will be forced to turn the matter over to Omar."

Sayed didn't bother to remind Yusuf that no name had been mentioned. Even if his bodyguard hadn't been keenly aware of Sayed's preoccupation with Aaliyah Amari, discovering the identity of the woman Sayed had spent the night with would not provide much of a challenge for the security team.

Sayed felt his own groan coming on.

"Is that what you want?" Yusuf asked when Sayed didn't reply to his statement.

No way would Sayed sic his father's *fixer* on Aaliyah. "That is not acceptable."

"As you say."

Which was not agreement. Not coming from the man who had grown up alongside Sayed and was almost as close as a brother.

Sayed had been trained to lead a country and Yusuf had been trained to protect the royal house of Zeena Sahra. They shared a common goal that had solidified the bond between them from childhood.

"I will see you shortly."

"As you wish, Emir."

Grinding his teeth at the additional sarcasm lacing his friend's tone, Sayed hung up the phone.

He turned to face Aaliyah. She'd scooted to the other side of the king-size bed and was sitting against the headboard, her long, dark hair in just-woken-up disarray, the sheet pulled up over her nudity.

The way it outlined her delectable curves, he did not think the cotton provided the barrier she thought it did.

There was no point putting off what he would

rather avoid altogether. "My bodyguard insists you sign a nondisclosure agreement."

Aaliyah nodded and then winced. Pressing the hand not holding the sheet in a death grip against the side of her head, she let her eyelids slide shut.

"You do not mind?"

"No," Aaliyah said in a whisper. "Would you mind not yelling, though?"

"You've got a hangover?"

Her eyes snapped open, fire sparking in their narrowed green depths. "Thank you, Captain Obvious."

He laughed, when he was sure nothing could have made him do so today. Not when he faced one of the biggest political crises of his life.

CHAPTER SEVEN

AALIYAH'S FROWN TURNED into a full-on glare.

And Sayed's laughter increased, lightness pushing away a layer of his stress. "You are a breath of fresh air."

"Why? No one else frowns at you?"

"It *is* pretty rare." He stood up, unashamed of his nudity. "Come. You can have the first shower. It will help."

She stared at him like he'd lost his mind. "I'll wait until you leave."

"Don't be ridiculous." He started going through the drawers and cabinets in the room. "Are there any pain relievers in the suite?"

"Your fian...the princess requested we stock ibuprofen. It is in the bathroom cabinet."

"She's not a princess," Sayed remarked as he went in search of the pain reliever. "Her father is a very influential sheikh, but he is not a king. And now she is merely a *Mrs. Palace Aid.*"

Which would not afford her any of the prestige or benefits life as *his* wife would have done.

"You're a little bitter there."

Coming back out of the bathroom with two pills and a glass of water, he shrugged. "She chose her life, now she will live it."

And he did not think the pampered daughter of a powerful sheikh would enjoy her newly humbled circumstances as much as Tahira clearly believed she would.

"Love makes up for a lot of deprivation."

"That is a sweet sentiment, but not very realistic." He handed Aaliyah the pills and water.

She frowned up at him. "My mother and I went without many luxuries you probably take for granted as necessities, but I never doubted her love and that made up for everything."

"She was no doubt an amazing woman," he said with sincerity.

Ms. Amari had raised Aaliyah, after all.

"She was." With a look of sadness, Aaliyah looked away as she swallowed the pills.

When she tried to hand him back the glass, he shook his head. "Drink it all. It will help."

"I don't think I can."

"Sip it."

She sighed. "It wasn't the alcohol, was it? You really are this bossy all of the time."

"It comes with the job." He smiled, the urge

to laugh again not easy to stifle, but he did not think she would appreciate it.

She finished the glass of water and put it down.

"Good. Now, go take your shower." If he timed it right, Yusuf would arrive while she was in the bathroom.

Sayed didn't understand this need he had to protect her, but he had no doubts it would embarrass Aaliyah greatly to face Sayed's security staff the morning after.

She seemed discombobulated enough by her one-night lover's presence.

She took a tighter grip on the sheet, her expression mutinous. "I'll wait."

"I am not accustomed to having my instructions disregarded," he told her, lacing his tone heavily with censure.

"Poor you." She appeared anything but sympathetic. "I'm sure you will survive it."

"You were not this stubbornly shy last night."

She glared up at him. "I was drunk."

"You told me you were not."

"I wanted you to make love to me."

"So, you knew enough to make the choice," he said with some relief.

"Of course. I'm not a child."

He tugged on the sheet. "Are you sure?"

Affront was written all over her lovely face.

He shrugged, lifting one brow. "Only, your refusal to get out of the bed seems a bit childish to me. After last night."

Color stained her cheeks, but determination firmed her chin. "Fine. Get me one of the hotel robes from closet."

"I assure you, I saw everything last night." He did not know why he was teasing her, but couldn't seem to help himself.

"It's not the same."

"No. You are right. We do not have the luxury of time to do anything about our nudity and the inevitable reaction to it this morning." He indicated his semierect sex with a small wave of his hand.

"Sayed!"

"What? You will not pretend you did not enjoy our lovemaking."

"Stop talking about it!"

"But why?" he asked in genuine confusion. "I do not mind telling you, it was amazing."

Yanking the sheet with her, she jumped up from the bed and wrapped herself in it before he got much more than a glimpse of honey skin and a couple of well-placed love bites he had very fond memories of giving her.

His breath expelled in a telling but unstoppable whoosh. "You are quite beautiful."

The rose of her cheeks turned crimson and

she scooted around him to storm across the room to the closet. Aaliyah pulled one of the aforementioned robes off its hanger and then stalked into the bathroom, attitude in every line of her body.

He watched her lovely form until it disappeared behind the firmly closed and—yes, he'd heard the snick—*locked* door.

His pang at the knowledge no woman in his life would react like she did was as inexplicable as it was undeniable.

A knock sounded on the door to the suite. Sayed donned the other robe from the closet, surprised when he realized that not only was it a man's robe with the dark blue hotel crest on the left breast, but it was his size.

Had the hotel anticipated him visiting his fiancée in the suite? The brand-new box of condoms in the bedside table would indicate a resounding *yes*.

Sayed let Yusuf in. "Leave my clothes in the other room and the agreement on the desk over there. She's agreed to sign it."

Subtle tension released from Yusuf's shoulders. "That is good."

"She did not balk at all."

"It would appear Miss Amari is a woman of principle."

"As I told you."

Yusuf disappeared into the other room as Sayed found himself gathering Aaliyah's clothing.

Considering her blushing reticence this morning, he did not think she would like to see their clothes strewn around the sitting room. They'd so clearly been yanked off their bodies in passion and with little finesse.

Yusuf cursed in the other room, a word usually reserved for serious screwups, which Sayed never indulged in.

The other man came storming back into the room. "Tell me the condoms are in the bathroom trash."

"What?" Sayed was used to the intrusiveness of constant security, but this was pushing the bounds of propriety. Yes, the condoms *were* in the bathroom trash bin.

That was something that Yusuf should take for granted. Sayed was not an idiot. "You forget yourself, Yusuf."

"No, *Emir*. That would be you."

"What are you talking about?" But even as he asked, Sayed's memory of the night before began to nag at him.

The final time they'd made love had been like waking from a dream. In fact, he was pretty sure that's how it had started. Bodies moving together

in the dark before waking to an unhurried joining and slipping back into slumber.

Sayed's insides tightened with realization.

*It hadn't been a dream and they hadn't used
a condom.*

"Since I doubt very sincerely you have suddenly developed an interest in rough sex, the
blood on the sheets can only mean one thing.
Miss Amari was a virgin."

What was Yusuf going on about? "What
blood?" Sayed's annoyance with himself made
his tone harsher than it needed to be.

"The smears in a single strategic spot on the
bottom sheet of the bed," Yusuf said, each word
an emphasized bullet.

Ignoring for a moment the other reality for
this new one, Sayed rushed into the bedroom,
his gaze falling on the telltale streaks almost instantly.

How had he missed them this morning? Oh,
yes, because he'd been so busy watching Aaliyah. Nothing else in the room had registered.

"She must have started." That would explain
her over-the-top shyness about exposing her
body to him this morning.

One of the things Sayed had enjoyed the most
about the night before had been Aaliyah's lack
of inhibition.

"Her period?" Yusuf asked giving the bloodstain a jaundiced look.

"What else?"

"What else indeed?"

"Anyway, we used condoms thoughtfully provided by the hotel." Except that one time, which he had no choice but to disclose.

"How could you be that careless?" Yusuf demanded, not unfairly.

Sayed could barely believe his own lack of control. "I woke from a dream that wasn't a dream."

"She was touching you?" Yusuf asked, his expression unreadable.

Another man might be able to refuse to answer such intimate questions, but Sayed had responsibilities that required a level of truthfulness with Yusuf he would never have offered even the close friend he was.

"Yes."

Yusuf did not comment. He did not need to. It was all written on the bodyguard's face.

He believed Sayed had been duped in a con as old as time, by a *virgin*.

Liyah took longer in the shower than she usually did, blushing as she washed the traces of blood from between her thighs. Even though there was no one else to see it.

She could not believe how abandoned she'd been with Sayed the night before. She'd brazenly initiated intimacy, even going so far as to touch him to wakefulness that last time.

She didn't regret it. She couldn't. It had been the most amazing experience of her life.

Even so, she was astonished at how she'd responded to Sayed. Yes, the whiskey she'd drunk had helped lower her inhibitions, but most of it was Sayed the man.

Not the emir.

She sighed. Her first waking moments had brought home very clearly that she no longer shared her bed with Sayed the man, but Sheikh Sayed bin Falah al Zeena, emir of his country.

Realizing she couldn't hide in the shower forever, she got out and dried off.

Bracing herself for another encounter with the emir, she wrapped her hair in a towel and donned the robe again. Liyah pulled the door open and came face-to-face with two men, not one.

Sayed's face wore a wary expression she didn't understand.

The other man was Yusuf, the same personal bodyguard that had been on the elevator with Sayed. And he was scowling. At her.

"I'm sorry I took so long." Embarrassment crawled up her insides. She hadn't meant to keep the emir from his shower. "You did insist I bathe first."

"Aaliyah, do you need Yusuf to get supplies for you?" Sayed asked.

"Supplies?" Had she skipped a page in the book?

"For your monthly."

Make that a whole chapter. Why would he offer such a thing? "No."

"Do not be embarrassed, Miss Amari," Yusuf assured her. "It is no trouble to procure what you need."

"I'm not even due for two more weeks," she blurted out, extremely uncomfortable.

She didn't know if Sayed's other lovers were just really open, or what, but Liyah found it very disconcerting talking about such a personal matter with him, much less in front of a virtual stranger. And she really didn't understand why it was coming up now.

Sayed made a sound that had her turning her attention to him. "You were a virgin," he accused, like it was a major crime.

Liyah stumbled back from his inexplicable but palpable anger. She ran into the jamb, her gaze skittering back to Yusuf only to find his scowl had grown darker.

"Why does it matter?" She could understand if he'd been disappointed in the sex, but his reactions last night made that unlikely. "I didn't lie about anything."

"You implied you were sexually active."

"When?" And again, why would it matter?

"When I told you about my *fast*. You said you hadn't been on one."

"You can't fast from something you've never had," she said with some exasperation.

Things started making sense, though. They were men from Zeena Sahra, the country that had spawned the attitude of Liyah's Amari relatives and her mother's own self-castigation.

Well, they could just get over themselves. Liyah *wasn't* her mother and her virginity, or current lack thereof, was *her* business, no one else's.

She drew herself up, pulling cool dignity into every pore. She would not be bullied. "My choice to give my virginity was and is *my* business."

"Are you saying you had plans to lose your virginity?" Sayed demanded.

"Of course not." What was the matter with him this morning? She was the one with the hangover. "You're the one who came to the suite while I was drinking," she reminded him. "I didn't have some great assignation planned."

"I came for some time on my own."

"And you found me." She challenged him with a look. "You didn't seem to mind that last night."

"That is not the issue here," he said frigidly.

"No? Well, my virginity is off the table of discussion."

"Miss Amari?" Yusuf asked, sounding slightly thawed.

Maybe he realized policing her morals wasn't his job.

She wasn't feeling the defrost, however. "Yes?" she asked, her tone the one she reserved for her peers who had thought their parents' money made them better than her.

"Are you on birth control?"

"No." Why would she be? She'd been a virgin.

Yusuf's scowl was back. "And yet you initiated sex without a condom."

Liyah wasn't sure if even last night's pleasure had been worth this kind of embarrassment. "We used condoms."

"Not the last time," Sayed said.

She stared at him. "What? No, that's not right. You always put a condom on before…"

Her discomfort at this type of discussion was only growing the longer it lasted.

"You woke me, it felt like a dream." He said it like he blamed her for that.

"This conversation is extremely uncomfortable for me. I do not know how it is in your families, but my mother discouraged talking about this kind of thing."

"By 'this kind of thing' do you mean sex, or the classic mantrap?" Yusuf asked with derision.

Liyah stared first at the bodyguard and then at Sayed. "Mantrap?" she asked, fury overcoming her embarrassment.

"What would you call it?"

"A mistake. *On both our parts,*" she emphasized, speaking to Sayed, though it was his bodyguard casting the slurs.

"A very convenient mistake," Yusuf opined.

She glared at him, but whatever she'd been going to say was preempted by Sayed.

"That is enough, Yusuf. You will apologize to Miss Amari for making that kind of accusation, as will I for allowing it. As she said, the mistake was mutual, though more my own than hers, considering Liyah's undeniable lack of experience."

Both men apologized with a surprising sincerity that allayed Liyah's anger, but did nothing to help her acute embarrassment.

"I accept your apologies. Now, can I sign that nondisclosure agreement? Only, I'd like to leave." She wanted out of this hotel suite and away from the emir and his bodyguard in the worst way.

Even if it meant saying her final goodbye to Sayed.

"Unfortunately, it is no longer that simple." Regret laced Sayed's every word.

"Why not?"

"You might be pregnant," he said, as if spelling it out for a small child, and not sounding at all pleased by the prospect.

She frowned. "I'm not stupid, but isn't that very unlikely?"

"Considering where you are at in your cycle, no."

"But…" She really didn't know what to say to that. She wanted to deny his assertion, but she couldn't.

Women had sex all the time without getting pregnant. Couldn't she be one of them?

The idea that she could be following in her mother's footsteps after a single night's indiscretion both terrified and dismayed her.

"Could we stop talking about this now?"

"You're acting very repressed," Sayed said, censure in his tone.

Ding. Ding. Ding. Give that man a prize. "Because I don't want to talk about this!"

"Last night's transgressions cannot be ignored."

Any fleeting sense of romance still lingering in her wary emotions from the night before dissipated then. "I don't talk about sex."

"Never?" Sayed's disbelief was palpable.

"No."

"But you are twenty-six and your mother died only recently."

"So?" Where did he think she got her discomfort with the subject from?

"What about friends?" he pressed, like it mattered for some reason she could not fathom.

"I was a scholarship student surrounded by peers who drove Beemers and wore designer jewelry with their school uniforms. I had very few friends, none I would have talked about regarding such a taboo subject."

Sayed was now looking at her strangely. "Sex is taboo?"

"Yes, which is why I wish we could stop talking about it right now."

"But last night..."

"Alcohol is apparently very effective at lowering my inhibitions."

"And in college?" Yusuf asked, still harping right along with his emir on the whole who-had-she-talked-about-sex-to thing.

"What part of 'taboo subject' are you not getting?" she demanded with asperity.

He shook his head, his expression pitying.

Which she would not accept. She'd never allowed anyone to pity her and Liyah wasn't about to start now. "I have hardly been deprived."

She'd had things a lot more important than

sex, or a romantic relationship, to think about. Namely, making Hena proud and proving Liyah's value as a student and later employee.

"Condoms are not infallible as birth control." Yusuf's frown was for both her and Sayed.

Sayed winced in acknowledgment and faced Liyah, his expression too serious. "The fact is, the nondisclosure agreement is the least of our worries right now, *habibti*."

"Don't call me that." It brought the night before into today where it had no place.

Yusuf sighed and looked very tired all of a sudden. "Miss Amari, you have to face reality. You may well be pregnant with the next heir of Zeena Sahra."

"No," she cried before panic had her spinning back into the bathroom and locking the door behind her.

Nausea twisted her stomach, chills rushing up and down Liyah's arms and legs. She could *not* be pregnant.

She was not her mother. Liyah had worked so hard to build a life her mother would be proud of. Hena Amari would be devastated by this turn of events.

The knowledge her mother was no longer around to witness Liyah's fall from grace was no comfort.

The fact she had no one to turn to for advice,

for support, even for a good lecture, sliced open
the wound of her mother's death that had barely
begun to heal.

This could not be happening. Liyah would not
allow it to happen.

She charged back into the room. Yusuf and
Sayed stopped talking and faced her, wearing
twin expressions of surprise.

"I am not pregnant. Do you hear me? *I will
not be pregnant.*"

Sayed's dark eyes widened, his features moving into lines of unwelcome sympathy. "It is not
something you can will away, Aaliyah, nor do I
believe you truly wish to."

"I was not setting some sort of *mantrap,*" she
all but shouted.

"I believe you. That is not what I referred to."

"What, then?" she demanded belligerently

"Would you will our child out of existence if
you could?"

She staggered back a step, her earlier nausea
returning. How could she answer that?

Of course she would never will a child out of
existence. She'd spent a lifetime believing her
father didn't want her, no matter what Hena had
tried to convince Liyah. She could never visit
that lack of acceptance on her own child.

Not even in the womb.

But there was another truth she could not ignore. "I do not want to be pregnant."

And she didn't care if those two attitudes seemed to be at odds. In her mind, one had nothing to do with the other.

If she were pregnant, she would make the best of it, but Liyah categorically *did not want to be* pregnant.

"Why did she have to die?" she asked of no one in particular, knowing only that she wanted to talk to Hena one last time with a pain that was tearing at her.

Sayed laid his hand on her arm. "I know you miss her, but your mother didn't leave you on purpose, *ya ghazal.*"

Liyah jumped, not having realized he'd moved so close. She looked up at Sayed, unsure why his words, his very presence, was so comforting. It shouldn't be. "Everything has been so hard since she left. Everything."

"It will be okay."

Confusion, grief and pain a maelstrom of emotion inside her, Liyah shook her head. "No. It can't be. The Amaris will know they were right to reject me. They'll want to take my baby away, too. She'll grow up without her father like I did."

Liyah's thoughts spun with dizzying speed, no chance for her to take hold of one.

"But don't you ever accuse her of blackmailing you," Liyah demanded fiercely. "Don't you dare pretend you don't remember me. You don't have to acknowledge her, but you won't treat her like that, like she's garbage under your shoe. Do you understand?"

CHAPTER EIGHT

"Perhaps I should get Abdullah-Hasiba," Yusuf said.

Liyah spun toward him. "No. You won't tell her. This is *my* business."

Her business. No one else's. She was alone now.

On one level, Liyah realized that she was flying apart, but she could do nothing to stop it. Her ability to repress her feelings and put on a cool front had deserted her completely.

After a wary glance at her, Yusuf looked toward Sayed for direction.

His emir ignored him, moving forward so Liyah had no choice but to back up until he had her pressed against the wall. She should have felt trapped, but her rampaging heart started to calm, her breathing slowing down to match his even inhalations.

He filled her vision and dominated her other

senses, leaving no room for anything else, including her escalating panic.

Cupping her cheeks, Sayed waited until Liyah met his gaze and held it. "Listen to me, *ya ghaliyah ghazal*. If you carry my child, we will face this together. You are not alone."

If only that were true. He could call her his precious gazelle, but she *wasn't* his. She *wasn't* precious to him.

No matter how beautiful he found her, women who didn't come from money or royalty, women like Liyah, who worked for a living, didn't exist for him in his world.

She almost laughed with gallows humor. "You don't even think I'm good enough for an affair. You aren't going to raise a child with me."

And why were they even talking like this. She *wasn't* pregnant. She couldn't be.

"I told you, the differences in our lives are just that. Not levels of superiority."

"Right. *Mrs. Palace Aid,* remember that?"

He huffed out a sound that was almost a laugh. "I believe that, after her betrayal, I am allowed a measure of leeway."

"I suppose."

"Just promise me this. We will take each day as it comes…together."

How could she promise that? How could she trust it?

"Promise me, *habibti*."

"You called me that on purpose."

"Everything I do is on purpose."

"Not taking my virginity, it wasn't."

Instead of renewing his anger with the reminder, it made him laugh. "No, perhaps not, but taking you to my bed was."

"You were drunk."

"No, I was not."

"Oh."

"Were you too inebriated to know what you were doing?" he asked. "Tell me the truth."

"No. I told you."

"Then we will both accept the consequences of choices we knowingly made."

She nodded.

"Together."

"For now."

"As long as your pregnancy is a possibility."

She tried to read his eyes, but could see nothing beyond sincerity and determination that might give her stubbornness a run for its money. "Okay."

He smiled. "Good. That is a beginning."

Yusuf cleared his throat. "We need to consider procurement of the morning-after pill."

Sayed turned so he stood between Liyah and the bodyguard, his back to her. "What are you talking about?"

"Emergency birth control."

"No."

"It's not—"

"An option," Sayed insisted, interrupting his bodyguard.

"It might be," Liyah offered, remembering an article she'd read about the different types of after-the-fact birth control. "If it's the one that doesn't get rid of pregnancy, only prevent it."

"How is it possible you know this and yet are so uncomfortable talking about sex?" Sayed asked, turning to face her again, his expression searching.

She rolled her eyes. "I read." One of her secret vices was a long-standing subscription to a popular women's magazine. "I'm inexperienced, not ignorant."

"Tell me about this pill."

"Well, there's more than one, but I think… hope…the one Yusuf is talking about is safe. You know, *if* I'm pregnant already, it won't hurt the baby. Or me." She wanted to keep denying the possibility she was pregnant.

And truly, she couldn't believe she was, but she wasn't an ostrich. She wouldn't be burying her head in the sand in the face of a potential reality.

No matter how much she might want to.

Sayed nodded acknowledgment. "It cannot be one hundred percent effective."

"Not absolutely, no."

"So, our immediate plans must be the same regardless."

"You are right, of course," Yusuf answered. "I will begin making arrangements."

"I'll have to talk to the local clinic about getting the pill."

"No," Sayed and Yusuf said in unison.

"What? Why not?" How else were they going to get it?

"Too risky," Yusuf said baldly.

"In what way?" she asked, again feeling like she was missing something.

Sayed grimaced. "We cannot afford for word of this situation to leak to the press, particularly in the wake of the scandal Tahira's defection has caused."

Liyah wanted to protest at being labeled a *situation,* but understood Sayed's viewpoint. He was already facing major public scandal; she had no desire to add to it.

"Stealth mode. I've got it."

Sayed sighed. "If destiny has ordained you carry my child, then we will do our best to face that fate with courage and honor, but we will proceed with caution in the interim."

"You make it sound like we're going to war."

He smiled and shook his head, dropping his hands. "Life is a war of choices, Aaliyah. Last night, neither of us made the best ones, but that does not mean we rush headlong into rash decisions this morning."

She missed the touch of his hands, but told herself not to be a fool. "We look at our options and take responsibility."

Something Liyah believed in very strongly and couldn't help being glad he did, too.

Sayed was no Gene Chatsfield.

"Exactly." Sayed's tone was laced with satisfied approval, his gaze almost warm before he turned very serious. "However, some responsibilities carry greater weight than others."

"What do you mean?"

"I need to return to Zeena Sahra. Tahira's actions will have long-reaching consequences for our country."

Feeling unaccountably bereft at the thought of his abandonment, Liyah nevertheless nodded. "I understand."

"Good. It is unfortunate you will not be able to work out your notice, but it is fortuitous that you already made your plans to leave."

"What? Why won't I work out my notice?"

"I've told you, we must leave for Zeena Sahra immediately."

"You said *you* had to leave."

He gave her a look that said she wasn't following him. "Naturally you must come with me."

"Why?"

"You may carry my child."

"But we don't know."

"And until we do, you will be under my protection and care."

"But—"

"Come, do not tell me you would not love to visit the country of your mother's birth."

"I would, very much, but under different circumstances than these."

He shrugged. "We make of our circumstances what we wish them to be."

"Remember that when you're dealing with the fallout from Tahira's elopement." Liyah felt bad as soon as she said the words. "I'm sorry. I didn't mean to make light of what you're going through."

"Apology accepted. Now, let us prepare for our trip."

"I didn't say I was going."

"But you will." He smiled winningly. "What better guide to introduce you to the magic that is Zeena Sahra than its emir?"

"I don't remember you being this persuasive last night." Bossy, yes, persuasive, no.

"It is another facet of my character for you to come to know."

* * *

As the jet taxied down the runway, Liyah marveled at how efficiently Sayed's people worked.

It was easier than thinking about *why* she was on this plane.

In the time it took Liyah to explain to the head housekeeper that an unavoidable circumstance had arisen which required Liyah to leave London immediately, they had packed her bedsit, paid off the lease and delivered her things to Sayed's jet.

She hadn't brought much more than clothes with her from the States to begin with, but still.

All this effort and near-frightening efficiency on behalf of the *possibility* she carried Sayed's baby.

Thankfully, her boss had been a lot more understanding than Liyah had expected. The head housekeeper had told Liyah that with her work ethic, the older woman knew her lead chambermaid would not be leaving if any other choice was open to her.

"My counterpart in San Francisco as well as your former employers had nothing but good things to say about you, Miss Amari."

The unprecedented warmth and affirmation from the usually no-nonsense woman had been a balm to Liyah's battered pride after her father's attack on her integrity the day before.

And it had made Liyah feel guilty because

she wasn't telling the whole truth and her only reason for having to leave was the results of her own poor judgment.

It was a smooth takeoff and it hardly seemed as if any time had passed at all before the pilot announced they'd gained sufficient stability and altitude to move about the cabin and turn on small electronic devices.

"I wasn't expecting that on a private plane," she said to Sayed, who sat beside her.

"Air safety regulations must be maintained." The answer did not come from Sayed, but Yusuf, who now stood in the aisle beside their seats.

He and the rest of the security team were sitting toward the front of the plane. Two on either side of a table they'd been using to play cards on since the door had been closed for takeoff.

Other than the cabin attendant, there was no one else on the spacious private jet. Clearly, Sayed was taking pains to keep her presence on the plane under wraps.

She should have felt like his dirty secret, but his attitude toward her was too respectful. And as she'd told him earlier, she understood the need for stealth mode.

For now.

She wasn't Hena Amari; Liyah wasn't about to fade into the background to save the man she'd had sex with from facing up to his responsibilities.

Sayed, who had taken the seat beside her rather than sitting opposite, had papers spread on the table.

They looked like printouts of news articles. Since most of them had pictures of Tahira and a rather ordinary-looking man, Liyah assumed they were the media's response to the elopement.

The man in the pictures with the Middle Eastern beauty did not appear near middle age, but his hair was clearly already thinning. Though there were stress lines around his eyes, they still appeared kind.

And Liyah thought she might understand how a woman could trust her life to this man over one who had never shown the slightest physical interest in her despite their engagement.

Because for all Tahira's beauty, *she* looked extremely young and even more innocent than Liyah had been before last night.

Sayed noticed her interest in the articles and waved at them. "My former fiancée with her *palace aid.*"

"You're going to have to stop putting that rather obvious emphasis on his job title if you don't want the media to label you an elitist."

Sayed frowned, but Yusuf said, "Miss Amari is right."

"You are not my public relations specialist," the emir reminded his bodyguard.

Yusuf didn't bother to answer, but held out a single pill blister pack. "As we discussed."

Sayed took it. "Thank you."

Yusuf nodded before returning to his seat.

Liyah did not watch him go; her focus was stuck on the silver packet in Sayed's hand.

"How effective is it?" she asked, her memory not very clear on that point.

"Dr. Batsmani said it is considered between eighty and ninety-five percent."

"Then why am I on this plane? Why didn't I just take it back in London and be done with it?"

"Five to twenty percent are hardly impossible odds." Sayed called the cabin attendant over for water with a wave of his hand.

When it arrived, Liyah opened the blister pack with inexplicable reluctance. Her head knew this was absolutely the right thing to do. She hadn't planned on motherhood at this point in her life, if ever.

If she were pregnant, Liyah would do her best, just as Hena Amari had done. That didn't mean she craved the opportunity to raise a child alone.

Although, according to Sayed, that was not one of the options she had to worry about.

Some little part of her heart disagreed with her head, telling her to forget the pill. Hadn't she wondered what kind of sane woman could let a man like Sayed go?

But no woman with honor would want to have him because he was trapped.

Besides, last night had been the first time she'd ever allowed her emotions to rule. And the aftermath had not been a resounding success.

"It has no effectiveness sitting in your hand," he teased.

She leaned toward him. "Shh…"

"It's just a pill. Nothing to be embarrassed about."

"You know what it's for," she whispered.

Humor, rather than the seriousness she would have expected, warmed his dark eyes. "Yes, indeed. I do know."

"I don't understand how you're so cavalier about…" She paused, looking for a word that wouldn't practically burn her mouth to say.

"Sex?" he asked, striving for innocent, but too amused to be anywhere close.

She glared at him. "You're from Zeena Sahra. You went without for three years. You should understand repressed."

"Suppressed, maybe. It's not the same. I am not ashamed to share a common physical need with an entire planet of people."

"It's different for you, you're a man."

"Do you think so?"

"Mom was pretty adamant that women had to remain chaste until marriage."

"And yet you decided not to."

"I doubt I'll ever marry," she admitted. "I'm too shy with men."

"Really?" He didn't sound doubtful, so she didn't take offense at his question.

"Most men. The combination of alcohol and you is a lethal combination."

"I would like to think the alcohol was unnecessary."

"It probably would be in future," she admitted with the honesty she seemed unable to suppress around him. "But last night? It definitely played its role."

"And yet you insist you were in control of your faculties when you chose to make love with me."

"I was, just not chained down by my usual inhibitions and introversion around men."

"You will be less nervous with the opposite sex in the future, I am sure." He didn't sound exactly pleased by that prospect.

"It didn't work that way for my mom."

"She had you."

"And a family who rejected her. I have no one left to reject me."

"That's a rather morbid thought."

"Sorry."

"I will reject you if it will make you feel better."

"Don't do me any favors." But she felt a small smile curving her lips.

She liked bantering with him.

Which scared her probably more than it should.

Determined to lead with her head, not her heart, she took a deep breath, tossed back the pill and swallowed it down with water.

CHAPTER NINE

As the minutes wore on, a need for the restroom broke through Liyah's consuming thoughts.

Loathe to interrupt Sayed in his furious typing on the computer he'd pulled out, she tried to ignore the growing urgency.

She grabbed a magazine from the pocket to the side of her chair and laid it on the table, hoping the glossy stories about other people's lives would keep her mind occupied and off her biological needs. She flipped through the pages, nothing catching her attention.

Shifting slightly from one side to the other helped, but pretty soon she was going to have to ask Sayed to move.

Suddenly, he stopped typing and leaned toward her. "Are you all right, *habibti?*"

"Yes, I just, um…" Liyah wasn't just repressed about sex, but found talking about any private bodily functions a trial.

Which was ridiculous, she realized. She was an adult woman, for goodness' sake.

"You should have told me you were a virgin." Sayed frowned at her. "I could have shown more restraint with you last night."

"Are you trying to undo a lifetime of repression in a single day, or something?" If asking him to move so she could use the restroom would have been embarrassing, this was mortifying. "I'm fine."

"You are clearly in pain."

"I need to pee," she huffed out in a furious whisper, frustrated by her own reticence and his insistence.

"Why did you not say so?" He rose, allowing her to exit her seat.

When she got back, she considered sitting across from him, but didn't gainsay him when he stood again so she could retake her seat by the window.

Once she was settled in again, he handed her an electronic reader. "It has most of the recent bestsellers, but if you want to download something else, the plane is set up with wireless internet."

"Thank you. The magazines would have been fine."

"Nonsense. Though, really, you should probably take a nap."

Startled, she asked, "I look tired?"

"Perhaps a little. It has been a full and wearing day."

He could say that again. "For you, too, but I don't see you dozing in your chair."

"The last time I napped, stuffed animals still decorated my bed." He smiled. "Getting six hours of sleep in a row is a luxury for me."

"But that's not healthy."

He shrugged. "Such is the life of an emir taking over the responsibilities of a melech with no younger brother to take over my own diplomatic duties."

"Why is your father abdicating? Does he have health issues?" she asked before realizing it was probably an invasive query. "Sorry, you don't have to answer."

"I never answer questions I do not wish to."

"Arrogance has its benefits."

He smiled. "I suppose so. I do not mind telling you my father is in excellent health."

"Is he tired of being king?" she probed, trying to understand the heavy responsibilities being thrust on Sayed.

"Not at all."

"Then why?"

"It is tradition."

"Will your father take over the diplomatic stuff once he's no longer acting melech?"

Sayed jerked, as if surprised by the question. "That would not be in line with Zeena Sahran tradition. I am not sure my father would find taking orders from his son a comfortable circumstance."

"But the melech dictates political policy?"

"With the help of a cabinet of counselors, yes. My father will act as one of my advisers, as well."

It still wasn't making sense to her. "So, what, your father is just going to retire and start golfing, or something? Won't he get bored?" How much time could it take to give Sayed advice every day?

Maybe she didn't understand working monarchies, but she could not imagine a former king content to sit home twiddling his thumbs.

"Honestly? I have wondered the same thing myself. My father is a very dynamic man and I do not think he would enjoy the pursuits that kept my grandfather busy in his twilight years."

"So, why retire now? Do you want to take over as melech?"

"No one has ever asked me that." He looked at her like she was some kind of rare species he'd never seen before.

"Maybe they should have. What's the answer?"

"My duty is clear."

"Yes, but is it one you want, or even need, to take on right now?"

"You question things you cannot hope to understand."

"Maybe." But he still hadn't answered the question and Liyah thought that was telling.

Sayed went back to his computer, dismissing her. Refusing to take it personally, Liyah skimmed his download of that morning's copy of *The Times.* He had probably been happy to note there was no mention of Tahira's elopement, but it would certainly be in tomorrow's edition.

After a while, she set the reader down, intending to take that nap he suggested.

But as soon as she closed her eyes, everything started pressing in on her. The argument with her father played over in her mind like an unpleasant reality show. When she managed to push those images aside, then pictures of the night before rose up to fill the void.

An unrelenting montage of the sensual and profound that uselessly fed her newly discovered love.

Sighing, she opened her eyes.

It didn't help. Her mind and heart were determined to dwell on emotions and experiences she would have been better off without.

Sayed turned from his work at his computer. "You are very pensive, Aaliyah."

"Don't you think I have reason to be?" She rubbed her temples. "I may not be an emir, but my whole life just took a ninety-degree turn."

"Perhaps you needed a detour."

"Do you think you know what's best for *everybody?*"

"It is in the job description."

"Right."

He smiled.

And she almost smiled back. Darn him.

That nap was sounding better and better. If only she could sleep, but then she'd probably dream about him. She'd done that *before* they'd made love. Now the dreams would probably be even more frequent and, with her new knowledge, definitely more graphic.

She expected him to go back to his work, but he didn't. "You said something yesterday about having a confrontation with your father being the reason you'd broken into Tahira's liquor stash."

Liyah opened her mouth to deflect, but she wanted to discuss the painful event with someone and Sayed was offering. "Yes."

"It did not go well?"

"No."

"You alluded to him treating you very poorly." Sayed's dark gaze probed hers.

"He did."

"You are being rather laconic." Sayed smiled, as if he found her amusing.

She didn't mind. She liked his smile. Too much. "I suppose I am."

She found herself grinning at his huff of obviously exaggerated exasperation, but then memories took away the lightness his humor had wrought. "It hurt that my father thought I was trying to work an angle, but that's not what was most painful."

"What was it, then?"

"When it became clear that my mom had lied to me my whole life." That had hurt so much. "She always told me that even though he could not have me in his life because he already had a wife and children, he cared enough to send a small stipend to help with my care and education."

"And this was a lie?"

"Yes. Oh, he was married, but he didn't even know I existed."

"That must have been quite a blow." Sayed laid his hand over hers, offering comfort she needed badly. "To learn your beloved mother had been dishonest with you, but also to be made aware that whatever concern you'd thought he had for you had no substance."

"You can't care about someone you don't even know exists."

"And then when he learned, he reacted badly."

"That's one way to put it."

Liyah wanted to lean into Sayed, but stopped herself from such a blatantly needy action. "The best I can figure out, the money Mom saved from not paying rent was what she pretended came from him."

It had been an elaborate but necessary ruse as Hena had insisted on teaching Liyah about finances from a young age. Her own parents had not been forthcoming with Hena and she'd made some bad monetary decisions in her ignorance.

She'd been determined her own daughter would not be put in the same situation.

Hena teaching Liyah about finances resulted in her daughter being very aware of their own. The pretense of support payments had worked to conceal both of the big secrets her mother kept from Liyah.

"Not paying rent?" Sayed asked.

"Another thing she hid from me. Her father owned our apartment and allowed us to live there rent-free as long as Mom promised not to bring me to Zeena Sahra."

"What?" Sayed's expression registered astonishment. "Why would he make such a stipulation?"

"So I wouldn't shame them with my existence."

"Because your mother chose to raise you," he guessed.

Apparently, he understood his own culture better than Liyah did. She'd never understand that kind of thinking. "Yes."

"Was that the reason you had no immediate plans to travel to Zeena Sahra?"

"Not on your life. Once I'd fulfilled my mom's last wish, I had every intention of visiting her homeland."

"You are very strong-minded."

"Another facet of my character for you to get to know," she said, facetiously repeating his words of the morning back to him.

He nodded quite seriously, though. "Yes, it is, and one I believe I like."

"Considering how bossy you are, that is difficult to believe."

He shrugged. "Nevertheless, it is the truth."

"You're surrounded by yes-men," she guessed, not sure she believed it.

"You've met Yusuf," Sayed said with meaning.

She felt another smile and gratitude for it. "He doesn't seem overawed by you, that's for sure."

"I assure you, he is not."

"That makes two of us," she said cheekily.

"I am wounded. A man hopes his lover esteems him."

"We're hardly lovers." They were more like a one-night stand with consequences.

His gaze heated. "I would like to be."

Suddenly tension thrummed between them.

"I find that hard to believe."

"I will not press my attentions on you, but I will also not pretend the thought of making love to you again does not dominate my thoughts far too much, particularly considering the issues facing me."

"You still want me?"

"Very much so."

"But won't that make the chances of pregnancy higher?"

"We will use condoms."

She blushed, as much at his frank speech as at the fact she hadn't immediately thought of that, as well. "Okay."

"Okay?"

"I want you, too." And any stored memory for the future she could manage to hoard, she would.

"I am glad."

"Me, too, I think."

They shared a look that made sitting in the luxury leather seat on the private jet uncomfortable.

She was pretty sure he would have done something about it right then, though she had no idea what it would have been considering their circumstances, but the flight attendant came over to set the table in front of them for dinner.

They were eating their braised lamb with potatoes and vegetables when he asked, "You discovered these things after your mother's death?"

Liyah found herself explaining how she'd found out her grandfather owned her apartment, how utterly devastating the funeral and meeting with the lawyer afterward had been when he had told her she must vacate her apartment.

"I didn't let them see it, though. I wouldn't give them the satisfaction."

"You have admirable emotional control."

If he realized the feelings she had for him she'd been unable to prevent or stifle, he wouldn't think so.

"Do you plan to return to San Francisco?"

"After we confirm I'm not pregnant?"

"If that is the case, yes."

"I don't know. Maybe I will travel for a while." She'd planned to save what was left of her mother's life insurance for the future, but to what end?

Liyah was twenty-six. If she didn't experience life now, when would she?

"Alone?" Sayed asked, disapproval evident. "Your mother would not encourage that, I think."

"I'm an adult and this is the twenty-first century, not the twelfth. A woman can travel alone."

"Not safely."

"Oh, please."

Sayed spent the next five minutes quoting statistics for crime against women traveling alone, particularly out of their home countries.

"Why do you know all this?"

"My cousin Samira wanted to go backpacking across Europe without bodyguard or chaperone a couple of years ago."

"How old was she?" He was thirty-six, Liyah knew. She couldn't quite picture a woman in the same age bracket wanting that kind of trip.

But then again, why not?

"Twenty-two. Her mother is my father's younger sister."

"And you said no."

"Actually, my father refused permission on the request of my aunt."

"Why not her own father?" Or Samira's mother, for that matter?

"Her father died in the explosion that killed my older brother."

"I'm sorry."

"It is an old grief."

"But not one that ever goes away completely."

"No."

"So, I bet Samira was mad." Or maybe being raised in the royal family had made it easier to accept restrictions for the woman who was four years younger than Liyah.

"We found her a well-trained female body-guard team and a companion to travel with her."

"And they went backpacking?" Liyah asked in shock. "Seriously?"

"With a few travel compromises, yes."

"Let me guess, they rode first class on the trains and had drivers in the cities they visited on a well-ordered travel itinerary."

He smiled winningly. "Something like that."

"So, is Samira your only cousin?"

"No, she has a younger brother. Bilal. My aunt was pregnant when she lost my uncle."

"Are you close?"

"He is twelve years my junior."

"I'm sure he looks up to you."

"I spent what time I could with him since moving back from the States, but he left for his own years at university. Bilal was to return to Zeena Sahra in time for my wedding." Sayed's lips twisted in a grimace.

"He is close with my father. He stepped in for his deceased brother-in-law from the beginning."

"Bilal is lucky to have you both."

Sayed shrugged. "He is family."

"So, why can't you train him for the emir responsibilities before taking over from your father as melech?"

"You do not think I will make a good king?" Sayed demanded, sounding hurt.

"That's not what I'm saying. I'm just pointing out there are options to tradition." Her mother's insistence on certain traditions had hurt Liyah more than helped her.

Hena's willingness to break with others had made Liyah's life what it was—in a very good way. Which was not to say that all tradition was bad, but being a slave to it was.

"Tell me about growing up in San Francisco," Sayed said in an obvious attempt to change the subject.

Liyah didn't hesitate, though. Because answering him gave her a chance to talk about her mom and that was something she'd been craving to do.

Sayed listened attentively to the stories of Liyah's childhood and time living with her mother as an adult.

"You clearly loved your mother very much."

"Yes."

"It is equally apparent that she loved you fiercely."

Suddenly choked with emotion, Liyah could only nod.

He narrowed his eyes in thought. "It sounds very much like each prevarication on your mother's part was done with the intent to protect your feelings."

"Then why ask me to find my father? She had

to know once I realized the truth how devastated I would be, how his rejection would hurt."

"I can only theorize Ms. Amari expected a much different reaction from your father than the one he gave you."

"She died hoping her family would one day acknowledge me."

"She was an optimist."

Liyah smiled. "She definitely was. She tended to see the best in people and dismiss their flaws." Expelling a long breath, she admitted, "I also don't think she ever stopped loving my father."

And because of that love, Hena Amari had built Gene Chatsfield up in her head to be a man very different than the one he was in reality.

"While that love may have been misplaced, your mother's love for you was not. You were undoubtedly the most important person in her life."

"She sacrificed so much for me and she never once threw it back in my face."

"A truly astonishing woman."

"Yes, she was."

"I think, perhaps, her daughter is a great deal like her."

Liyah wasn't sure how true that was, but if she could share her mother's strength and willingness to sacrifice for others, she would count herself very blessed.

"You have already shown how deep your well of integrity goes," Sayed remarked.

"How so?"

"Many women would have tried to capitalize on what happened last night. You've done nothing but try to help me mitigate any possible negative consequences."

Liyah couldn't believe how much better she felt about everything that had happened since her mother's death after talking with Sayed. "Thank you."

"No thanks needed. We all need a friend now and again."

"Do you have friends? People *you* can trust enough to talk to?"

"I have my parents and Yusuf. Perhaps Bilal will become one now that he will be back in Zeena Sahra."

"That is a short list." Even with his cousin added to it.

"Trust for a man in my position cannot be offered on a whim."

She could well imagine. Last night would not have helped with that, either. "I'm sorry."

"For?"

"Last night."

"I am not." He shrugged. "I should be, but I enjoyed it too much to allow for genuine regret."

He sounded like he thought that was a terrible weakness.

"You're awfully hard on yourself."

"My father says I feel the weight of the world on my shoulders."

"Not carry?"

"No. He insists I do not need to carry the burden of responsibility that I do, but one day soon, I will rule in his place when I was never meant to do so. For his sake and that of my brother, I can offer nothing less than everything to my country."

A brother's death in childhood would have been devastating to any child, but for Sayed and the way it changed the course of his life? Even more so.

Looking into eyes filled with gravity to match his declarations, Liyah felt a twinge of emotion she refused to call love. "Maybe you *are* a little awe-inspiring, anyway."

"I am glad you think so." He grinned, the expression so unguarded it took her breath away.

CHAPTER TEN

"So Gene Chatsfield was your mother's lover?" Sayed asked, sounding pretty sure of her answer.

"Yes."

"I imagine he has reasons for his distrustful attitude," Sayed said mildly.

She still frowned. "But I wasn't lying to him."

"You and I know that, but he did not."

Sayed's belief in her honesty helped soothe the sting of her father's blatant rejection and hurtful accusations.

"He didn't even remember what she looked like," Liyah said, still unable to grasp that particular reality.

How could he have forgotten such a special, wonderful woman?

"It sounds like he was in a bad place in his life when they met," Sayed said, as if reading Liyah's thoughts.

"That doesn't excuse him seducing an innocent young woman and then forgetting about her as if she never mattered."

"Many errors in judgment cannot be excused, but that does not mean they can never be forgiven."

"So, you're going to forgive Tahira?"

"Eventually," he said, shocking Liyah. "But probably not until everything her defection has caused has been dealt with, and in a way that is not to the detriment of my people."

"Wow, you really are some kind of amazing." Though she had no doubt he meant his caveat for forgiveness one hundred percent.

He looked pleased by her declaration. "I have very good parents."

"I think your basic core has a lot to do with it, as well."

Sayed shrugged. "Perhaps, but even in that I must acknowledge the gift of good DNA."

She reached out and touched his face. She simply couldn't help herself.

He stilled, making no move to dislodge her hand. "What?"

"I just wanted to reassure myself you're real."

"I am flesh and blood like the next man."

"Emir."

"With you, I prefer to be a man only."

"Is that possible?" Her heart responded to the

man, but her head reminded her that the emir was way out of her league.

"Right now, in this moment, it is."

Neither broke eye contact as the attendant cleared their dinner detritus from the table.

"Did you know there is a small bedroom in the back of the plane?" he asked when the attendant had moved away. "It is a necessary luxury for those times when travel and sleep schedules do not coincide."

Goose bumps were traveling up her arm from the circling of his thumb against her palm. "Um, that's nice?"

"Would you like to see it?"

Liyah was being propositioned. She wasn't sure who was more shocked when she accepted.

Herself, or Sayed.

Sayed led Aaliyah into the sleeping quarters. Although it was as superbly appointed as the rest of the plane, the bed was only a double size.

He would not allow the cramped quarters to prevent him from his current objective: giving Aaliyah an experience worthy of the gift of her innocence.

No matter how mind-bogglingly good the sex had been the night before, they'd both been under the influence of alcohol. And he hadn't known she was a virgin.

He'd entered her body completely unaware of the gift she bestowed. Without proper care many virgins experienced a great deal of pain their first time.

It was only by grace and benevolent genetics that Aaliyah had not.

The knowledge he was her only lover resonated in the most primal part of Sayed's psyche.

And he wanted more.

Desire riding him harder than a runaway camel in the desert, he reached for her the moment the door shut behind them. Sayed pulled Aaliyah flush with his body and into a kiss. Over half a foot shorter than him, she should not fit so perfectly, but she did.

Like their two bodies had been made just for this connection.

He demanded a response from her and she gave it, her passion a match for his, though expressed differently. Her lips melted under his, parting almost instantly. Without a second thought, he accepted the alluring, silent invitation.

Surprised and a little worried that it was every bit as stunning as the night before, he rubbed his tongue along hers.

She tasted so sweet, familiar in a way that should not be possible after only one night together.

Her hands came up and then his *egal* and *keffiyeh* were being tugged off in one motion and tossed away.

Amused despite the desire raging through his body, he broke the kiss. "You do not want the emir?"

Emerald eyes trapped his with the emotion glowing in them. "Sayed, when we are like this, I will always want the man."

"No one wants only the man." Not since the day he became emir, not merely second son and sheikh.

"I do," she vowed, her musical voice vibrating with sincerity. "I did last night."

"No matter what we might wish, I never stop being the emir." It was a warning for him as much as her.

His future had been written in the stars the day his brother was killed. Sayed was not just a figurehead.

He had no choices about walking away from his responsibilities. There was no one to take his place and he loved his people too much to let them down.

She shook her head, looking up at him, her beautiful oval features set in serious lines. "You're right and you're wrong at the same time. Because right now, you *are* Sayed. Yes, you are emir, but that is not *all* you are."

He wished he could agree, but honesty forced him to shake his head in disagreement, even as his hands smoothed down her body, seeking the hem of her top.

"What do you call Melech Falah?" She shivered as he tugged her blouse out of her waistband.

"Father."

She rubbed her cheek against his affectionately. "So, he is not only a king, but he is your dad, too?"

"Yes, but his duty comes first."

"Are you sure about that?" she asked, shifting her lower body against his.

Did she expect him to focus on *conversation* right now?

She laid her hands against his chest, one landing unerringly over his heart. "You don't think it would have been better for Zeena Sahra's sense of country unity and its international consequence for their prince to be educated and raised within its borders?"

"My safety was necessary." There was no sentimentality in that.

"Oh, yes, absolutely, but your dad sent you away. The king would have just increased your security. How often did he and your mother come to visit you in the U.S.?"

"Several times a year." Though Sayed had

only been allowed home a few times in all the years he attended school in the States.

They'd spent the summers together in Europe with his aunt and young cousins, their exact location kept from any but his father's closest advisers.

"Tell me again, your father was never more or less than melech."

"He was and is my *father,*" Sayed said, never having denied it, but also understanding she had a point in what she said.

"And right now? You are my *man, rohi.* Even if it is only for the next hour, I won't give up a second of that and I won't let you, either."

"I am supposed to be the experienced one here, but you are seducing me utterly." He could not acknowledge the *my soul.*

No doubt she had heard it from her mother and did not realize the deeper connotations the endearment carried between lovers. Those implications were all too fitting between them, though he would probably never have the freedom to acknowledge.

But their souls fit, just like the rest of them.

"I like that." She pushed his outer robe off his shoulders. "Because everything about you makes me want you more."

He did nothing to stop the gold-trimmed black fabric from pooling at their feet.

She went directly for his suit jacket, taking time to lay it over a chair in the corner. "I may be repressed, but you dress like a monk."

"I do not think monks wear Armani." And she did not seem very repressed right now.

"Maybe not." She grinned up at him cheekily. "I'd rather you weren't wearing it right now, either."

Delighted by her, he laughed. "Your wish is my pleasure to grant."

He finished undressing, not minding in the least that she seemed intent on helping him.

When he was totally naked, his swollen sex jutting out from his body, he let her look her fill. He'd noticed how much she enjoyed it the night before. And having her gaze on him with such innocent hunger turned him on like nothing else.

She didn't even wait for him to suggest she join him in his nudity before she started stripping, too.

Primal masculine satisfaction coursed through him and he grinned, even as his body reacted to every inch of honey skin she revealed.

"What?" his undeniably proactive lover asked as she laid her oh-so-conservative skirt on the chair with his clothes.

"It is me, not the alcohol."

"What?" she asked, her expression confused as she unbuttoned her simple white blouse.

"Repressed Aaliyah has abandoned you for the present."

Her hands stilled, the blouse gaping to reveal the luscious curves of breasts in another very feminine bra while a blush climbed her throat and up into her face. Yet she didn't pull the open edges together.

"I feel free with you, like I can do anything and it's okay." She sounded astounded by that reality, but not unhappy.

He was delighted. "Exactly. Me. *Not the alcohol.*" *He* made her lose her inhibitions, no whiskey needed.

Her gaze sharpened in comprehension and she smiled. "Evidence would be in your favor."

"I am aware."

"Your arrogance is showing again."

"You say that like it's a bad thing."

Her smile made his heart pause in its beats.

He shook his head. "You have no idea what you do to me."

"I think I have a clue, *rohi.*" She gave a significant glance downward.

Laughing, he bent and swept her into his arms, pulling her scantily clad body flush to his.

He had never had so much fun with a lover.

She gasped, then threw her head back and hooted, the sound of amusement so sweet it sent shivers through him.

"You sure you don't make a habit of this?" she asked, still giggling. "It's just that it feels like a habit."

"Only with you."

He arranged her on the bed, having pulled the bedding back much to her apparent amusement.

"You find this funny?" Arousal was his predominant emotion at the moment, his sex so hard it was already leaking preejaculate.

"This? As in making love? No. But seriously, it's like you're a professional at the suave lover thing."

"At least you didn't compare me to a musical genre again."

"I couldn't have been too drunk if I was able to come up with metaphors."

"Or only a very inebriated woman would make such a comparison."

"There is that." She winked at him. "I stand by it, though."

"Tonight, you are not under any influence but me."

"I'll tell you a secret," she whispered against his ear as he settled next to her, leaning down with the intent to kiss her again.

"Yes?"

"You're a lot more intoxicating than that stuff I was drinking last night."

"And I will not leave you with a hangover."

"Just muscles sore in all the right places."

"I knew it." He sat up.

She grabbed his arm, like she thought he was going to leave. "What?"

"I *did* hurt you last night."

"What? No. Maybe a little, but isn't it always like that the first time?"

"Oh, no, it can be much worse. We were very lucky your body's barrier was not too stubborn." If it had been he might have noticed it, though.

All he'd felt was how tight she was, how good her silky, wet heat felt around his shaft.

"I wouldn't know about anyone else, I only know that last night was the most amazing experience of my life."

"Then the bar is high."

"For what?"

He worked on the remaining buttons of her blouse. "To make this time truly memorable and worthy of your first experience with a lover."

"Why?" she asked as she tugged on his arm.

Unable to deny her, he leaned down and took the kiss he'd meant to a moment ago. Her lips were soft under his, but she wasn't passive by any stretch, her mouth mobile and enticing.

He finished undoing her buttons and pulled her blouse from her body, lifting her to sit up so he could get it off completely. Feeling like he was opening a truly stunning gift, he took the opportunity to dispense with her bra, as well.

He loved the way her entire body shivered as her nipples were exposed to the air. She'd done the same the night before and he'd found it incredibly arousing. He still did.

Soft sounds came from her as he laid her back on the bed, this time coming down beside her fully. Naked skin slid against naked skin, building the intensity between them.

His hand resting possessively on her belly, he remembered her question and broke the explosive kiss. "Because that is what you deserve."

"Huh?" Unfocused green eyes looked up at him. "What?"

"Why I am committed to making this time better than last night."

"Oh, that's sweet," she said on a hitching breath as he began to caress her. "But unnecessary, not to mention unlikely."

"You think so?"

"Last night was pretty special."

"Tonight will blow your mind."

"You're kind of competitive, huh?"

He shrugged. He wasn't competitive so much as he always won. He was emir; he had to be the best at everything he chose to do.

It wasn't just built into his position; it was in his DNA.

"Can I touch you?" she asked, her voice husky with need.

"Of course."

She licked her lips. "Anywhere?"

"Yes." The word ended on a hiss as her small hand curled around his sex.

She made a hum of approval as her grip moved up and down the column of hard flesh, driving his arousal higher and higher.

"Do not stop," he instructed her as he began his own explorations.

He intended to drive her to the point of madness with desire.

Long pleasurable minutes later, he realized that every moan of pleasure he pulled from her, every restless movement of her body, drove him closer to the edge of losing his own control.

He'd never found it so hard to hold back, not even the first time he'd lain with a woman.

But Aaliyah Amari was some kind of sensual sorceress, every sexy whimper a powerful spell on his body.

Even when he pressed her legs apart and put his mouth on her, his own body reacted like she was touching him.

She cried out, tried to pull away. "No. That's… I don't think…"

He lifted his head. "Do not think, *habibti*. Feel."

He tasted her, the sweet tang of her arousal exploding on his tongue as the scent of almonds mixed with musk created a heady perfume around him.

Each woman had her own unique scent, but he had never found one so alluring.

He pushed his tongue inside her and pulled it out again, kissing her in ultimate intimacy.

She mewled, but when he shifted his head so he could flick her clitoris before circling it with the tip of his tongue, she screamed. Long and loudly.

Her responsiveness was addictive and he went back again and again for more of her taste, more of her reactions, using his tongue to lave and then caress with his consciously hardened tip. He added a finger to her passage, reveling in the slick wetness he found there.

She moved against him, her sounds growing more and more desperate, her muscles contracting and relaxing until she went rigid and came. Her thighs locked on either side of his head.

He did not mind at all. He had no intention of moving.

He softened the caress of his tongue, though, pulling his finger from inside her, drawing out her pleasure but not to the point of discomfort.

She went rigid once more and then completely

boneless, her legs flopping down to leave her completely open to him.

It was time for the next step: rebuilding her sexual need until she was whimpering for release.

And that was exactly what Sayed did, touching his *habibti* all over with hands first, but then his mouth—using teeth and tongue to bring her back to the edge of exploding.

However, by the time he rolled on the condom he had to be careful not to come from his own touch, and that never happened to him.

He wished they didn't need the barrier. Making love with nothing between them had been one of the most profound experiences of his life, even if he'd thought it a dream at the time.

Perhaps it was better this way.

Sheathed to prevent the further sharing of his seed with her body and perhaps keep back some part of his soul from hers, he turned her onto her side and angled his body behind her.

"What are you doing?" she demanded, her voice heavy with passion. "I *need,* Sayed."

"And I will give you what you need." He pressed into her from behind, the position allowing him to touch her at will.

One arm tucked under her neck so he could reach her breasts, he reached down with his other hand to touch her clitoris as he began to move.

She gasped out sexy demands even as she moved her pelvis with instinctive rhythm.

This time they came together, their shouts mixing in a sexual song he could easily become seriously addicted to.

The thought was so disturbing, he did not let himself sink into afterglow. He took hold of the condom and carefully pulled out of her, but could not make himself move away completely.

She made a distinctly unhappy sound.

"Shh…" He kissed her sweaty brow, the affectionate gesture too natural to be comfortable for a man who knew his time with his love would be measured in days not years. "I need to take care of the condom."

He made his way to the efficiency-size en suite on unsteady legs.

The mirror showed him a face he'd never seen before, one with eyes far too soft with vulnerability.

He was emir. Not merely a man.

Not a man at all who could afford to crave a woman like he'd learned to hunger for Aaliyah after such a short time.

He needed to find himself and put this other man away. Sayed owed it to his people and to the brother who had died before getting the chance to lead them.

Sayed should have been working strategy the

whole plane ride, but he'd spent hours talking with Liyah and then making love.

He had to put distance between them, or he wasn't going to be able to do what he needed to when the pregnancy test came back negative.

Let her go.

CHAPTER ELEVEN

QUEEN DURRAH ESCORTED Liyah to her quarters in the palace harem herself.

Even the melecha's personal attention could not mitigate Liyah's feeling of abandonment upon Sayed's nearly instant disappearance after their arrival to the palace, however.

Sayed had barely taken the time to introduce her to his esteemed parents before excusing himself to speak to his father privately. The monarchs had been surprisingly gracious, but Sayed's desertion had stung.

Coming on top of the way he'd been acting since they made love, it was doubly hurtful.

He'd walked into the bathroom a man and came out one hundred percent emir, focused on affairs of state.

Sayed had dressed in silence and then turned to her, his gaze set firmly somewhere beyond her left shoulder. "Nap now. I'll have the cabin attendant knock on the door in time for you to shower and dress for landing."

She might have argued if her eyes hadn't already been drooping, her body seconds from sliding into sleep regardless.

As he'd promised, she'd been alerted in time to shower and dress in clothes miraculously ironed while she'd been napping. However, even though she'd returned to her seat, Sayed had spent the entire descent and landing talking to Yusuf, who had joined them in one of the empty seats across the table.

Then Sayed had been fully occupied the drive to the palace with his smartphone.

Liyah knew he had important issues that had to be dealt with, but that hadn't diminished her sense of the growing distance between them.

A distance that should never have been bridged in the first place, her brain tried to remind her. Her emotions foolishly balked at that truth.

Liyah had never warred so much within herself as she had since meeting Sayed, not even when she'd been deciding about going to England to meet her biological father.

No matter how unreasonable, how hopeless, how *ridiculous,* her growing feelings for Sayed were, Liyah could not deny them. However, she had no intention of sharing them with anyone else, especially the man himself.

Not by word, or deed.

Which meant she maintained her outward dignity and self-possession with particular care as she kept pace with the queen.

She led Liyah up a grand staircase that made the one at the Chatsfield London seem simple and unassuming in comparison. A strip of plush red carpet ran up the center of the mahogany steps shined to a glasslike finish. The matching elegantly carved banisters were held up by over a hundred ornate three-foot-high crystal newels.

Everything about the stone palace complex located on the shore of Zeena Sahra's Bahir Sea was over the top and yet not in the least tacky.

After several turns and traversing a distance easily equal to a couple city blocks, they approached an imposing set of double doors. Liyah wasn't even surprised to find a man dressed in the manner she'd come to associate with Sayed's security detail standing to the left of the doors.

The queen nodded to him, but made no verbal greeting.

The guard opened the door on the right and Queen Durrah led Liyah through it, only the softest swishing sound indicating it closing behind them.

Queen Durrah smiled at Liyah, her amber gaze reflecting an impressive determination and confidence of spirit. "For the next five days, you will stay here as our honored guest, but your name and relationship to my son will not be revealed."

She did not ask if Liyah understood, or even agreed. Somehow that assumption of agreement was more intimidating than Sayed's bossiest moments.

"Five days?" Liyah asked.

"Perhaps six."

Liyah nodded, though not entirely sure why that exact length of stay was necessary.

"The definitive blood test can be performed five days after the *event* at the earliest." The queen waved her hand as if referring to something she would prefer not to address directly.

The pregnancy test.

"Do you want me to stay in my room?" So much for Sayed's promise to be her tour guide.

"My goodness, no." The queen opened a door on her right to reveal a lovely sitting room done in champagne with burgundy accents. "You are not a prisoner here."

Just a guest who had to remain anonymous.

Liyah could not quite suppress how impressed she was by her accommodations. They could have put her in the servants' quarters and she would not have minded at all. "This is the size of the living room in our old apartment."

"Our?" the queen asked in a way Liyah found she could not refuse to answer.

Not that she would have regardless. "I shared an apartment with my mother until her death four months ago."

Liyah managed to speak of her mother's loss without revealing what it cost her to do so, but she turned away to give herself a moment. Though she hoped her intent was not obvious. Liyah would not have Queen Durrah thinking she was some weak emotional mess.

"I am very sorry to hear about your mother." There was no mistaking the sympathy in the older woman's tone. "I remember losing my own mother. I miss her to this day."

"Thank you," Liyah replied, renewing her attempt to pull in her emotions.

"Aaliyah." There was a command in the queen's tone Liyah once again could not ignore.

She turned. "Yes, Your Highness?"

"I am not accustomed to speaking to the back of someone's head." The queen shook her head, her eyes narrowing. "Never mind. Did my son suggest you should stay in your room during your stay here?"

"No."

Queen Durrah nodded as if approving Liyah's response. "While you are not a prisoner, there are a few concessions we will all appreciate you making."

Liyah was impressed. The queen hadn't ordered her to make those concessions, but her wording made it clear she expected Liyah's co-operation.

"Whatever I can do," she promised the other woman.

"While your things have been delivered, during your stay here we would prefer you not wear the clothes you brought with you. You will discover traditional Zeena Sahran clothing in your wardrobe. You may consider it a gift and take it with you when you leave the palace."

"That is not necessary." She hadn't missed the queen's certainty Liyah wouldn't be staying.

"Nevertheless, the clothing is yours. We would appreciate it very much if you would wear it whenever you leave this room, including the hijab over your hair."

"Okay."

"You may notice I do not wear the hijab. It is by no means a requirement in our culture." The queen wore her hair in an elegant coif, a tiara that could have been a large hair ornament tucked into the dark tresses.

"I don't mind wearing the hijab." Though Liyah didn't really understand why Queen Durrah had asked her to do so.

"I am glad to hear that, but it is absolutely not a requirement." Sayed's deep masculine tones thrummed through Liyah, drawing her around to face him with inexorable pull.

"Sayed." Liyah was incapable of further speech at the moment.

"Do you like your suite?"

She nodded. "It's beautiful."

"But not her prison," Queen Durrah inserted.

"Of course not, Mother. What have you been telling her?"

"We have just been discussing how best to handle her visit."

"I believe I said I wanted to have that discussion with her?" he asked, irritation sparking in his dark gaze.

The queen shook her head. "You should not be here at all."

"And yet you knew I intended to come and speak to Aaliyah as soon as I'd talked to Father."

"Surely you could not be finished discussing your strategy for dealing with Tahira's little escapade already?" the queen prompted.

"We can finish after I've made sure Aaliyah is comfortable."

"Surely I am capable of doing that."

Tired of watching words being bounced between mother and son like tennis volleys, Liyah went out on the balcony and left them to it.

Sayed joined her a few seconds later. "Are you all right, Aaliyah?"

"Do you want a polite lie, or the truth?"

"Truth, please." His hand landed on her shoulder and Liyah wondered what the queen thought of that.

"I'm a bit overwhelmed, and while this suite is gorgeous it *does* feel a little like a prison."

He turned her to face him and waited until she tipped her head back so their gazes met. "It's not meant to. If nothing else, I want you to enjoy your stay here, to truly come to know the country of your mother's birth."

"Will I see you at all?"

"You are seeing me now."

"That's not an answer."

"It's the best one I can give you." The glimpse she got in that second of Sayed the man, the very conflicted man, told Liyah she wasn't the only one struggling with their situation.

"You promised to be my tour guide."

"And so he shall be." The queen stood in the open French doors leading to the balcony.

"Mother, could you please give us some privacy?" Sayed asked in a pained tone that would have been funny if Liyah wasn't feeling so fragile.

More emotions she was doing her best to hide.

"I'll just call for some tea and wait for it in the sitting room." Whether it was the queen's not-so-subtle way of telling her son she wasn't leaving them entirely alone, or a simple peace offering, Liyah wasn't up to guessing.

"Aaliyah, please."

"What?" she asked, searching the depths of Sayed's brown gaze for something.

Even she couldn't say exactly what.

"Don't look like that."

"Like what?" She was doing her best not to look like anything.

He dropped his forehead against hers, breaking eye contact, but cocooning them in another type of intimacy. "Like you might break."

"I won't break."

"Promise me."

"I promise." Though she wasn't sure she was telling the truth. And she was an honest woman. "I'll try."

He made a sound that hurt to hear. "Taking it one day at a time, right?"

"Does that really work?"

"Yes." His hands cupped both sides of her neck, his thumbs rubbing softly against her skin.

Knowing if she didn't break contact she was going to say or do something she'd regret, she stepped away. "I suppose it's a good philosophy but not one I think you exercise very often."

He took a step toward her and then seemed to think better of it and moved even farther away.

"You would be surprised. No matter how

much a planner you are, in the world of politics and running a country there is only so much you can control." He managed a contained tone, but his hands fisted the wrought-iron railing in front of him with white-knuckled intensity.

"Then you cannot blame yourself for what is beyond that control." She hoped he took the words as the absolution she meant.

He swallowed, and when he spoke again his tone was a little ragged around the edges. "Cultivating the patience to deal with challenges as they arrive instead of fighting against them is another thing my father taught me was essential."

They remained there, together but silent, until the queen informed them that the tea had arrived and the king had requested his son join him to finish their discussion.

Seeming unable to help himself, Sayed kissed Liyah on the temple before leaving her suite.

Despite the fact even this small display of affection was not exactly acceptable by Zeena Sahran standards, the queen did not remark on it as she poured Liyah a cup of steaming jasmine tea.

"Now, about the hijab."

"Yes?"

"Wearing a scarf gives you instant access to an unremarkable assurance for privacy of identity should it become necessary." Queen Durrah smiled very much like her son. "Besides, there is less chance of you being recognized as a foreigner if you wear one."

"And the clothes?"

"Hiding in plain sight." The queen smiled. "I believe that is a well-known technique, yes?"

"Yes."

"The presence in the palace of a traditional Zeena Sahran woman would be cause for much less speculation than an obvious American."

Liyah didn't doubt it, having to bite back a smile at how much the queen reminded her of Sayed in that moment. They were both so certain they knew what was right.

"Unfortunately, there is nothing we can do about your Americanized speech."

"I'm perfectly happy to speak in Arabic while staying here at the palace," Liyah said in a perfect Zeena Sahran dialect.

The queen's eyes widened and then she flashed that smile so reminiscent of her son again. "How wonderful. Sayed did not mention your fluency in our language."

"I've never mentioned it." Liyah smiled herself as she explained. "My mother spoke only the Arabic dialect of her homeland in our home and expected me to do the same."

"Perhaps we'll wait to apprise Sayed of this," the queen offered with a surprising glint of mischief in her eye.

Bewildered by the melecha's quicksilver mood change, Liyah nodded. "You're really different than I expected."

"Sayed did not get his propensity for impetuous action from a stranger." Queen Durrah winked. "I've decided I like you."

Ignoring the claim that could have little weight, Liyah stared at the older woman with an expression she knew revealed disbelief. "You believe your son is impetuous?"

"Less now than he was as a child, yes, but your presence here is proof he has not eradicated the trait entirely."

"You do not sound too upset by that." Another conundrum for Liyah's brain.

"I am not. Sayed is emir and will one day be melech, but he is still my son. His brother's death changed him so much, it changed all of us." For a moment grief shimmered in the depths of Queen Durrah's gaze. "It pleases me to see proof he has not changed completely."

"So, you're not upset about this situation?" Liyah found that hard to believe.

"What will be, will be."

"But surely you don't want me to be the mother of your grandchild." Though the older woman had already made it clear she didn't expect Liyah to be pregnant.

The queen reached out and patted Liyah's arm.

"As to that, I cannot say. I may instinctively like you, but we have barely just met. One thing I'm certain of, your presence here will shake things up."

"And you think that's a good thing?"

"Oh, yes. Both my husband and son are still living in the shadow of Umar's death, though it occurred more than twenty years ago. I will miss my son every day until we are reunited in the afterlife, but it is time my family moved into the future."

Liyah understood that sentiment, though it had only been a few months since her mom's death. If Sayed hadn't come crashing into her life, Liyah was pretty certain her own life would have slid into marking time as she grieved a circumstance that could never be changed.

"Don't you think Tahira's elopement was enough of a shake-up?" Liyah had the temerity to ask.

"Certainly that was the catalyst for change. I find it very interesting that my son's response was to engage in shockingly unprecedented and personally perilous behavior with you."

Liyah had no answer to that.

Queen Durrah's beautiful face settled into thoughtfulness. "Honestly, I expected Tahira's betrayal to entrench him even more firmly behind the walls he erected so many years ago. I am very happy to be wrong."

Liyah paced her suite, having just returned from late-morning tea with Queen Durrah.

Who, despite her royal status and very definitive views on propriety, had turned out to be both likable and kind. And very much interested in her son's happiness.

Liyah had been astonished by the warm reception she'd received from both the king and queen. She threatened their well-ordered existence and Liyah's presence could do nothing but add to issues caused by Tahira's defection.

Yet both the monarchs had treated Liyah with nothing but respect. The king was a little more standoffish, but she didn't find that surprising. The fact he treated Liyah like a welcome guest to the royal palace did.

Queen Durrah had gone one step farther and taken pains to spend time each day with Liyah, however. Sayed's mother seemed intent on developing a friendship with the hotel employee her son had temporarily plucked out of obscurity.

The melecha had managed to ferret out the details of Liyah's estrangement from her Amari relatives in the mere two days since her arrival in Zeena Sahra. A very restful person with a smile very similar to her son's, Queen Durrah had found her way into Liyah's affections almost as quickly as Sayed had.

His mother had unequivocally denounced the actions of Liyah's relatives, remarking that someone needed to speak to them and bring them to awareness of the error of their ways.

The rather fervid gleam in Queen Durrah's amber gaze had given Liyah pause, but thankfully no rapprochement with the Amaris had been attempted.

Not that a queen would bother herself with the personal affairs of someone like Liyah, but for a moment there...well, Liyah had worried.

A knock sounded on the suite's door and she quickly pulled up the beautiful hijab that matched the pale green silk *dishdasha* she wore. The emerald-green embroidery around the hem and over her bodice was the exact shade as the chiffon of the hijab.

Liyah had never felt so feminine and pretty as she did since coming to Zeena Sahra. Gone were her conservative suits and boring white blouses, replaced by *dishdasha* gowns and *kameez* in vibrant colors Liyah never would have chosen for herself.

But she liked them. A lot.

She'd always dressed plainly, in clothes that did nothing to accentuate her feminine curves. While the traditional *dishdashas* and *kameez* were considered more modest than western clothing, the long dresses and long tunic-style tops with matching pants Liyah had found in her wardrobe were cut to emphasize the fact she was a woman.

The swish of silk that accompanied her every movement further increased her sense of femininity.

Not that Sayed had noticed. He hadn't had an opportunity to because she hadn't seen him for even the briefest glimpse in the past forty-eight hours. During the one dinner she'd shared with his parents, he hadn't been there.

At her own request, she ate breakfast alone in her room and lunch in the harem garden. But if he had invited her to share one of those meals with him, she would have been happy to do so.

Liyah wasn't surprised at the neglect. She'd seen Sayed's war within himself on the day of her arrival. She thought he might be the one person of her acquaintance less willing to give in to emotions than she was.

Adjusting the hijab, she pulled the door open and found a familiar face on the other side. "Abdullah-Hasiba! Come in."

Liyah stepped back to let the older woman into her suite, but Hasiba shook her head.

Her expression did not reflect Liyah's delight

in their renewed acquaintance. "My melecha has requested your presence."

"Yes, of course," Liyah replied.

Hasiba spun on her heel, walking away without another word and Liyah's happiness deflated as quickly as it had come.

She followed the longtime family retainer in silence, saddened by the clear end to a friendship with a woman she admired.

Hasiba stopped outside a familiar set of double doors, one of many in the palace complex she'd discovered. "My melecha awaits you inside."

Liyah nodded, unable to speak. Why she should react so strongly to this small rejection when she'd faced much worse ones, she didn't know, but the loss of Hasiba's regard hurt.

Hasiba huffed, like she was annoyed, which she probably was.

Liyah reached for the door handle but the older woman's hand beat hers, covering the brass knob. "You took advantage of my emir."

"I didn't." Liyah had no defense but the truth.

"He was an engaged man."

"No. Tahira eloped."

"You could not have known."

Suddenly Liyah understood the root of Hasiba's disappointment in her. "I did know. I overheard the emir talking about it with Yusuf on the elevator."

"My emir would never show such a lack of discretion."

"They weren't conversing in English, but honestly? I don't think either of them realized I was there. You must realize how blindsided he was by Tahira's actions."

Hasiba's expression turned even darker. "So, you thought you'd trap yourself a sheikh now that he was single?"

Liyah opened her mouth to reply, anger overcoming her sadness, but a masculine voice beat her to it.

"I assure you, Abdullah-Hasiba, Miss Amari has in no way attempted to *trap* me," Sayed said, distaste for the idea ringing in his tone. "She could certainly have taken advantage, but did not and has done everything she could to diminish the consequences of *my* folly."

Liyah should have asserted claim to her part in their joint debacle, but she was too busy drinking in the sight of Sayed after a two-day drought.

"I apologize, my emir," Hasiba said with apparent sincerity. "I made assumptions I should not have." Then she proved her earnestness by turning to Liyah. "I am truly sorry, Liyah."

Liyah nodded. "Your reaction is understandable." Mostly. Liyah wouldn't lie to herself and pretend the assumption of such things about her character didn't hurt.

She hated the fact that because some people would take advantage of a man in Sayed's situation, anyone would just assume Liyah would, too.

"I do not agree," Sayed said, his tone icy.

Hasiba flinched, clearly upset she'd angered her emir.

Liyah gave the older woman a small smile. "Don't worry about it, really." She frowned up at Sayed. "Don't be cranky. Hasiba's heartfelt loyalty is a gift you should not take for granted much less criticize her for."

"Obviously you two are friends—does she not owe you loyalty, as well?"

"Over her dedication to your family? Not even. Be reasonable, Sayed."

Hasiba gasped at Liyah's familiarity with her sheikh, but she did not comment on it. Thankfully.

"I am always reasonable. My emotions do not rule me."

Liyah got the additional layer of message in his words and took it to heart, feeling inexplicably buoyed by the idea he felt something toward her, even if he did not intend to act on it. She was in the same frame of mind, wasn't she?

"Her Highness has requested Miss Amari's presence." Hasiba dropped her hand from the door and stepped back. "I will leave you to escort her inside."

Sayed frowned. "You called her Liyah just a moment ago."

"Yes, and in private consultation with your mother, I have leave to call her 'my lady,' but it would not be proper to refer to her with such familiarity in the company of others."

Looking unconvinced, Sayed nevertheless nodded and dismissed Hasiba. "Why did she call you Liyah?"

"That is what everyone calls me."

"You never gave me leave to do so." He made no move to enter his mother's private reception rooms.

"I like it when you use my full name."

"Oh, yes?" Again, he didn't appear completely convinced.

Liyah sighed and admitted, "Only my mother ever called me Aaliyah. It was special to me."

His handsome face filled with satisfaction. "Then I am honored to be in her company."

Sayed was grateful for the looser conventions in his country than many surrounding Zeena Sahra when Liyah laid her hand on his arm at his invitation.

Just that much connection helped soothe the ever-growing need to touch her, though what he really wanted was to kiss her senseless.

He opened the door to his mother's private reception room and led Liyah inside.

"Good, you have both arrived." His mother's pleased expression made him immediately nervous.

"Good afternoon, Queen Durrah." Aaliyah smiled at his mother, but did not step away from Sayed's side.

And with unfamiliar weakness, he was glad.

"Good afternoon, dear. I thought you might enjoy a tour of the capital today." His mother gave him a look of censure. "You have not yet left the palace."

"I thought it was for the best." Aaliyah's reply told him nothing of how she felt about that.

And though she was undoubtedly right, he did not like the fact she felt constrained to remain in the palace.

"You are not our prisoner, as I have stated before." His mother turned an expectant expression on Sayed. "Is that not right, my son?"

"Yes, of course."

"Good. You can accompany Aaliyah. Who better to share the history and points of interest of our beloved city?" she asked, unconsciously echoing his unacted-upon invitation to Aaliyah.

"But I have—"

"Nothing on your calendar for this afternoon,"

his mother interrupted him with uncharacteristic lack of tact.

If his schedule was clear, this was the first he'd heard of it. Which meant his mother had arranged the break from meetings.

She was committed to this course of action.

Even knowing the futility of arguing, he still had to try. "I am the last person that should be seen with Aaliyah."

"You brought her as a guest to our home, did you not?" his mother asked, her tone a mixture of censure and steel-hard determination.

"You know I did and that I had little choice in it."

"Regardless, she is your guest and you have shamefully neglected her the past two days. You were not raised to display such a lack of consideration."

"This is hardly a normal circumstance."

"Circumstances are rarely *normal* in the life of a royal, Sayed, as you well know."

"And if we are seen together?" he challenged. This was not a good idea. She had to see that.

"What if you are? I am certain it will not be in a compromising position. It would do your image some good to be seen with such a lovely companion after Tahira's defection."

"But the media will speculate as to her identity."

"I would recommend taking an unmarked car

on the tour," his mother said dryly. "And offering no one Aaliyah's name."

"My keeping company with a hotel maid will cause a scandal and we do not need another one of those." He'd spent the past two days working nonstop to put a lid on the one they were facing already.

"It was my understanding that she was a floor supervisor?"

"On the housekeeping staff." How could his mother not see what a disaster waiting to happen this outing was?

"Do not be a snob, Sayed. It is unbecoming."

He wasn't sure which bothered him more, his mother's words or the fact that Aaliyah had dropped her hand from his arm and taken several steps away from him.

"I am not." He turned to Aaliyah, uncaring for the moment if his mother understood his thoughts.

Aaliyah's feelings were uppermost in his mind right then.

She'd made an effort to school her features into an emotionless mask. However, it did not hide the hurt deep in her emerald eyes. Not from him, anyway.

He moved toward her, drawn by an irresistible need to wipe that pain from her gaze. "Aaliyah—"

"Don't." She put her hand up. "Whatever you

think you need to say, don't. While I appreciate Queen Durrah's concern for my entertainment, I am *not* your guest."

Aaliyah sidestepped, managing to put more space between them and move closer to the door. "I am not your friend. You have absolutely no obligation to spend time with me. There is no reason for you to give up your afternoon."

"My son is a better host than that," his mother inserted firmly.

Aaliyah shook her head, giving his mother a sad little smile that made him want to swear. "While I appreciate your earlier offer of a car and driver and this latest attempt to provide me with a tour guide, in three days we'll do the blood test and discover I'm not pregnant."

Regardless of words that sounded heartless as his own mind replayed them, Sayed wanted to protest. He was fighting what felt like a hopeless rearguard action to emotions he could not allow himself to feel.

Oblivious to his conflicted thoughts, Aaliyah continued, "Then I will move to a hotel and explore my mother's homeland to my heart's content. Until then, I am fine with not leaving the palace and making as little impact here as possible."

"There is no reason for you to be sequestered in the palace, much less the harem."

"I mean no offense, but I'm afraid I must disagree, Queen Durrah. Sayed is right. There is every reason. If you don't mind, I'll go back to my room now. I downloaded a new book on the reader Sayed gave me."

"How generous of my son to provide you with books to read," his mother said, sarcasm making her usually soft tones clipped.

Aaliyah just shrugged and left without waiting for either he or his mother to dismiss her from their presence.

CHAPTER TWELVE

"WELL DONE, SAYED," his mother mocked.

He turned quickly to face her, angry in a way he never was with his beloved parent. "Why would you suggest something so fraught with risk? And if you were going to do so, you could have at least given us both the courtesy to approach me without Aaliyah present."

His mother stood up, her expression filled with censure and unmuted disappointment. "Because it never occurred to me that you would lack any courtesy whatsoever and make it so obvious you did not want to spend time with that poor girl. She is here because of you, or had you forgotten that salient fact?"

"It was a one-night stand."

"Was it?"

"Of course, what else could it be?"

"A gift of fate?"

"How can you say that?" He spun away, his emotions in turmoil he did not want even his mother to see. Especially when she was voicing thoughts he'd done his best to suppress in his own mind. "There can be nothing between Aaliyah and me."

But the words rang hollow, even to his own ears.

"Because she doesn't come with a breeding certificate and border treaty as Tahira would have done?"

Shocked by his mother's attitude, he blurted, "I am an emir."

Though that mattered less and less with each passing day. Aaliyah had connected to Sayed the man and respected the prince. What more could he want from his emira?

His practical brain had no answer.

"I thought sending you to school in the States would curb some of that elitist mentality."

"I am no elitist." He didn't like the sensation of having the same argument with his mother as he'd had with Aaliyah.

"Perhaps not, though evidence would suggest otherwise. You are, however, undoubtedly an idiot." Affection in her tone dulled some of the sting of her denouncement.

He turned back to face her, only to watch as his mother left the room, throwing both doors wide.

"She always was good at the grand exit." His

father stood near the door leading to an adjoining room.

Sayed dry-washed his face with his hand. "Yes."

"She has also always been very intuitive. If she is pressing you to spend time with Miss Amari, perhaps that is what you should be doing." Was it possible his father agreed with Sayed's mother?

Maybe the melech didn't realize how close to gone on Aaliyah his son, the emir, was. "Why? So I can get into yet another weeklong wait to discover my fate?"

"You are that attracted to her?"

"I wanted to snatch the birth control pill from her hand and throw it in the garbage rather than let her take it," Sayed admitted.

He'd wanted to just let destiny take its course, but a prince could not deny his responsibilities. Sayed thought Yusuf might have realized it, too, but like a true friend, he'd said nothing.

"I am surprised," his father admitted, sounding it.

"No more so than I."

"Your mother and I were betrothed in the cradle."

"I know."

"But I was in love with her before our wedding ever took place."

"You were?" Sayed could not stifle his shock. "You married so young."

"From the moment I began to notice the opposite sex, Durrah was the one I wanted. Discovering on our wedding night that she shared my affection was the happiest moment of my life to that point."

"You were very lucky."

"Blessed by fate," his father agreed with a rare genuine smile. "Yes, we were."

"Mother was everything that you could want in your queen." With nothing in her background for the media to feast on.

Not like Aaliyah, who not only came from the masses but whose mother had not been married to her father. Sayed did not care, but some would and she could be hurt deeply by the viciousness the media was capable of.

"Yes, she was and is."

"I barely know Aaliyah," Sayed claimed, though he wasn't sure he spoke the truth.

He felt like he already knew the important parts of her too well to forget easily.

"You knew Tahira your entire life."

Sayed wasn't sure what point his father was trying to make. "And I had no idea she was having an affair."

"You cannot be sure she was."

"She ran off with him."

"For love, if her note to her father is to be believed. I raised you better than to simply assume the worst on the basis of circumstantial evidence."

"Yes, you did."

"And I raised you better than to hurt someone the way you did Miss Amari arguing with your mother about spending time with her." His father frowned. "Didn't you tell me you promised to show her the country of her mother's birth?"

"It was a foolish promise to make."

"But a commitment nonetheless." The implacability of his father's tone and expression said this was not an argument Sayed had a hope of winning.

Especially when it meant fighting his own deepest desires.

As he went to leave his mother's receiving room, his father's voice stayed him at the door. "It may help to remember a salient truth, Sayed."

"Yes?"

"Both your mother and I have already committed to accepting and helping Aaliyah succeed in her role should she be pregnant."

"And if she's not."

"You know us well enough to answer that."

Sayed wasn't so sure. He'd only come to realize very recently how mistaken he'd been about himself. He'd thought he would have been content to marry Tahira and only now realized how miserable he would have been.

He thought he might even owe her a thank-you for the elopement.

Standing on the balcony overlooking the harem gardens, Liyah ignored the second knock on her door in less than hour.

Hopefully, if she didn't answer, whoever it was would take the hint and go away.

The sound of a door opening and soft footfalls across the carpet told her she had not been so lucky.

"I was an ass."

"Yes." She wasn't going to deny the obvious.

Nevertheless, Liyah did not react outwardly to Sayed's presence or his surprising admission, though her heart started beating faster.

Honestly, if she could ignore him completely right now, she'd prefer it.

But Sayed was a guy who took responsibility and apparently his mother believed he had some sort of obligation toward Liyah. Queen Durrah had apparently convinced her son of it, too.

So, here he was. To apologize? To invite Liyah on an outing?

Whatever it was, she wanted it over and him gone. Her defenses were always at her lowest around this man and she did not want him to see the tears tightening her throat.

He stepped up behind her, laying his hands on her shoulders. "I hurt you."

She shrugged, unwilling to lie and equally loath to admit to her weakness. It was too close to admitting why she was so susceptible to him.

Love hurt. There was no other name for the conflagration of emotion he sparked in her. She loved him.

She was pretty sure she always would, too. That one-true-love stuff she'd always thought a ridiculous fairy tale? She was living it. Only the happily ever after? It was still in the realm of fantasy and always would be.

"I am very sorry. It was not intentional." His right hand slipped down and around to press against her stomach, guiding her body back toward his.

"I never thought it was." She was just a one-night stand that wouldn't go away and his apology didn't change that, but she'd still liked hearing it. "Please let go of me."

She couldn't blame him for not wanting to spend time with her, but his touch brought her emotions too close to the surface. And that was something she couldn't deal with.

His lips brushed against her temple. "I want

nothing more than to spend the afternoon with you."

"Right."

He gently but firmly turned her to face him. If she could believe the evidence of her eyes, his expression showed turmoil equal to Liyah's. And this time, he was doing nothing to hide it.

It shouldn't matter, but it did. Forcing her gaze straight ahead, she opened her mouth to demand again he let her go, but she could not make the words come out.

She wanted this closeness.

He sighed, his hands rubbing in circles on Liyah's back. "I have spent the past two days putting out fires Tahira's elopement sparked. We have two border countries offering a similar alliance, accepting either one of which would lead to a dangerous political imbalance and almost certain aggression on the part of the other."

Did he even realize he was still touching Liyah?

"Tahira's country should be offering reparations along with the previously agreed-upon treaty, but her uncle's current strategy is to lay blame for her defection at my door."

Liyah had stubbornly kept her gaze on his chest, but she had to see what he was feeling about that. She raised her head, their gazes clashing immediately.

A volatile mix of emotions poured through her, needing the smallest spark to send them burning sky-high.

Longing. Love. Desire. Need. Pain. And worry.

Because he had major stress lines around his beautiful brown eyes.

Of its own volition, her hand lifted to smooth away those lines. "Sounds tense."

"That's one word for it. I have others that aren't acceptable in mixed company."

"Is it going to be okay?" Was *he* going to be all right?

"Yes, because there is no other option."

"Are you going to marry someone from those other two countries?"

"No."

"What about Tahira's country. Maybe she's got a sister? A cousin?"

He shook his head. "Right now the idea of a politically motivated match is leaving a very bad taste in my mouth."

"That makes sense." Liyah did her best to ignore her heart's leap at his pronouncement.

"So, with all of this to occupy my thoughts, you'd think there was no room for anything else."

"You don't have to make excuses for not seeing me. Your mother is kind, but she's wrong.

You don't owe me anything." Maybe if Liyah kept saying it, he'd realize she believed it.

No matter how much the truth hurt.

"I wasn't trying to excuse myself. I was admitting that even with everything else on my mind right now, I cannot stop thinking about you, craving you."

"You mean sex." Disappointing, but not unexpected. And it wasn't as if she'd say no. Surely he had to realize that.

"That's definitely part of it, but I *want* to take you sightseeing."

"You said—"

"A bunch of camel dung, because facing what I want doesn't mean I get to have it."

"You're kind of complicated."

"I'm an emir, complicated defines my life."

"Is there something we could do that wouldn't put us at risk for exposure?" She felt like a fugitive in witness protection asking, but as much as he was now disparaging his own arguments, he'd been right.

Having her recognized with him wouldn't do him any favors. Not because she wasn't good enough, but because—like he'd said before—she was just too different to fit in with his life.

She ignored the tiny voice that said she'd been fitting in pretty well with his family the past two days.

He smiled. "You are willing to spend time with me, even after I behaved like such an ass?"

"Yes." A smile played around her own lips. "But we have to stay in stealth mode."

If she had a chance to spend time with him before the inevitable and growing-closer expiry date of their association, she'd take it.

"We could go into the desert. Our family has been going to the same retreat since the first melech."

"Like your Camp David?"

"If Camp David stepped out of an *Arabian Nights* fantasy, yes."

"Really?" She made no effort to hide her enthusiasm.

"Absolutely. Will you come with me?"

The spark of uncertainty and steady burn of desire in his espresso gaze decided her. "Yes."

"Pack a bag. We'll spend at least one night."

"Can you afford to take this time off?"

"Taking myself out of the equation for the moment will actually make it easier for my father to effect his own form of diplomacy."

"That sounds ominous."

"Not really, but he yells a lot more than me. He can posture without me there as a witness to force the others to draw a line in the sand."

"Not a hard thing to do in the desert."

"But sandstorms have a habit of obliterating those lines."

"And Melech Falah is the sandstorm?" she asked.

"Yes."

"Then what are you?"

"The voice of rationality everyone will want to deal with after three days of my father's chest pounding."

"It's good cop/bad cop."

"On an international scale, yes." He grinned, clearly pleased with himself and his father.

She couldn't help returning the smile.

Sayed hadn't been exaggerating. The royal family's retreat *was* like a set from *Arabian Nights,* only every silk hanging and antique Turkish carpet was genuine.

They spent three days exploring the desert, Sayed showing Liyah the beauty of his country in his own unique way.

And they made love. Often and in romantic settings she would never have envisioned.

The last day, he took her to an oasis where he had a semipermanent tent set up. He said the herdsmen used it, but when he took her inside it smelled of sweet jasmine and was filled with silk blankets and pillows.

She twirled around, her silk *abayah* flowing gently around her. "This is no herdsmen's tent."

"No, today it is the tent for the emir and his lover."

She didn't deny the label like she might have three days before. Their affair might be short-lived, but she would never be the same and she didn't think he would, either.

They made love that night into the wee hours. Stars glittered in the cornflower-blue sky as they cuddled, facing the pulled-back curtains of the tent opening.

Security guards were in smaller tents around, but she'd learned to forget they were there. Strange how quickly a person could become adjusted to things like that.

She curled around his body, his arms holding her with fierce possessiveness and a sense of security no weaker for its lack of permanence.

"When is the blood test?" she asked.

"Dr. Batsmati will draw a sample tomorrow morning."

"And the blood test is one hundred percent accurate?"

"This one is, yes. It's why we had to wait a minimum of five days from making love."

"Then I guess I'll move to a hotel soon."

"You are assuming it will be negative."

"Aren't you?"

"No," he said, shocking her. "I've prepared for a positive result."

"What do you mean? What will happen if I am pregnant?" The question *was* academic as far as she was concerned.

Her body had already started responding as it usually did the week before her period.

"A royal wedding."

"What? What are you saying? We aren't getting married." Considering her feelings for him, she should have been thrilled at his words, but panic made her heart race instead.

She didn't want him trapped into marriage.

"If you are pregnant with my child, it is the only course of action open to us."

"But I took the pill. I'm not pregnant."

He shook his head. "One thing you learn in high-level politics is how real a chance even five percent, much less twenty, can be."

"But marriage? You can't be serious."

"Never more so." He looked down at her, his expression too shadowed to read in light provided by the moon and stars. "Don't you want to marry me?"

"That's not the point."

"No, it is not. The point is that you will not raise our child alone."

"Why can't we share custody? I could move to Zeena Sahra." There was nothing to return home to. No one who would care if she made her life halfway around the world. "There are hotels there. I could continue to build my career."

"And be what to our child?"

Was that a trick question? "Her mother."

"How do you propose to do that without causing a great scandal?"

"And you don't think marrying me—a chambermaid—would do that?"

"Lead chambermaid," he said, proving he remembered their first meeting. "And something more when you weren't taking a job to provide you access to your father."

"You're still nowhere near my orbit, you said so yourself."

"There will be a media furor." He sounded way less bothered by that than he should be. "But nothing like the ongoing existence of a woman in my son's life who is not my wife."

"You can't want to marry me. I'm not princess material at all."

"I disagree. You have already proven to have more heart and honorable intent than Tahira ever did—at least where I am concerned. You are articulate and intelligent, self-controlled, as well. Once you have the proper training, the rest of the world will be able to do nothing but admire my choice in emira."

"Proper training?" she asked carefully, not liking the sound of that at all.

His thumb caressed her palm, sending shivers through her. "Consider it like going to university to get a degree in being a political figure."

"A political figure's wife, surely."

"Make no mistake, as my emira and ultimately melecha of our country, you would have a political role, just as my mother does."

"How am I supposed to train for something like that?"

"With the teachers who served me best."

"You had tutors? I thought you went to boarding school in the States."

He smiled, the expression impacting her like it always did. "I'm referring to my parents. Both have already agreed to do their best to help you learn your new role, should it become necessary."

"I didn't think having sex with you was signing me up for a new career."

Sayed shrugged, his body shifting against hers. "Life is like that, full of curve balls, as one of my old professors was so fond of saying."

"This is crazy. You know that, don't you?"

"Difficult? Perhaps. Crazy? No."

"Stop talking about it." She wasn't pregnant and all this talk of marriage was only going to make it harder to leave him.

She couldn't afford dreams with so little substance.

"For now." Sayed turned over, pushing her onto her back and proceeded to blow her mind. Again.

If his lovemaking seemed to be tinged with desperation, she figured maybe her own feelings were simply reflecting back on her.

Sayed stormed into his father's office and threw the newspaper in his hand onto the king's desk. "Why didn't you tell me?"

"Once the story broke, there was nothing you could do." His father flicked a glance at the image of Sayed and Liyah in a passionate lip-lock—and not the first one in three days to run in their country's most widely circulated newspaper. "The only course of action left open was to wait and see how it was received."

"Pictures of Aaliyah and I kissing were on the Net hours after we arrived at the retreat."

"You did kiss her outside."

"In our private gardens!"

"Not that private." His father seemed a lot less angry than Sayed would have expected. "You know how dangerous a high-powered camera lens can be."

"How did they know we even left the palace?"

"You know we have media watching us all the time."

"Not this closely. Someone had to have leaked something."

His father shrugged. "Perhaps. Our people love the Cinderella angle. Have you noticed? Omar said it's all over the social media sites."

"And your *fixer* did nothing to kibosh it?"

"On the internet? Not going to happen."

"I doubt very sincerely the border countries looking for an alliance are nearly as caught up in the romance of it all," Sayed fairly growled.

"You would be surprised."

"What do you mean?"

"Apparently, none of them wanted us making such a firm alliance with the others. You marrying an outsider with no political agenda will actually work in our favor."

"Who said anything about marriage?"

"Do you really think anything else will suffice after that?" His father pointed to the second photo in the story.

It was of Sayed and Aaliyah leaving the oasis tent, his arm around her, their expressions and manner clearly that of a couple who had just made love.

"What if she won't agree?" Her reaction to Sayed bringing it up in response to her pregnancy had been a solid wall of negativity.

He hadn't realized how much he needed her to want it until she'd made it clear she *didn't*.

"You'll have to convince her. From the look of things, it shouldn't be that hard."

"You have no idea."

Liyah hung up with Dr. Batsmati, a tight band of disappointment squeezing her chest. They'd done a rush on the lab results.

He'd only drawn her blood a couple of hours ago. She wasn't pregnant.

Pretty soon, she'd be leaving the palace.

And she'd never see Sayed again.

Pain ripped through her as she'd only felt once before. When her mother died.

The rejection of her Amari relatives and her father hadn't been pleasant, but neither had caused this devastating depression to settle over her.

Even her mother's death hadn't made Liyah wonder if she would ever truly know joy again. Melodramatic?

Maybe, but she loved Sayed and she didn't care if it made sense. It didn't matter that she'd always thought it impossible to fall so deep so fast.

She'd done it and wasn't sure if her heart was going to survive the blow of losing Sayed.

And yet the temptation to leave without seeing him again was strong.

Only, she wasn't that person, the one who hid from the hard things in life. Hena Amari had set a better example than that.

Taking the time to change into a dark teal *dishdasha* Sayed had found particularly alluring, Liyah mentally prepared for the discussion to come.

She brushed her hair out until it shone and then draped the hijab over it loosely, framing her face to its best advantage.

Okay, so maybe she wanted Sayed to be at least a little sorry to say goodbye to her.

Opening the door, Liyah jumped back with a surprised squeak at the sight of Sayed there already, his fist raised to knock.

"Surely the sight of me is not such a shock," he said with one of the smiles she'd started to think of as hers.

He never offered that particular expression to anyone else that she'd noticed. And Liyah had been looking.

"You know this is the harem. You aren't supposed to be here."

"I am emir."

"And you still have to maintain traditions. What, is there some kind of secret passage you use, or something?" She really didn't think Sayed walked by the door guard without a qualm.

Dark color slashed Sayed's cheeks above his closely cropped beard. "Yes, in fact, there is."

"What? Really? Where? Show me." She was perfectly willing to be sidetracked from the discussion they had to have.

He laughed and shook his head. "You are pretty irresistible when you're all enthusiastic."

"So, show me."

"After we talk."

All anticipation drained away and she turned from him. "Dr. Batsmati called you, too. I thought he would."

"Actually, I haven't spoken to the good doctor." Sayed's gaze probed hers, stripping her bare if he but knew it. "Is this rather depressed appearance because he told you there was no baby, or that you *are* pregnant?"

"I'm not depressed," she lied.

"Uh-huh."

She flopped down onto the settee, no longer concerned with presenting the best image of the "one that got away" and equally uncaring about the secrets of the palace.

Did any of it really matter? "I'm not pregnant."

"And you are unhappy about that," he said, as if feeling his way toward something.

She sighed, tempted to lie again, but the man knew her more intimately than anyone else living. He would be able to tell. "Yes."

"Because?"

"Does it really matter?"

"Oddly enough, it does. You see, we are in something of a predicament." He dropped a newspaper onto the open seat beside her. "If you are unhappy at the thought of never seeing me again, all may not be lost. If you're simply feeling baby fever, that's another thing. Although it could work to our advantage, too."

"What in the world are you talking about?"

He indicated the paper with a nod of his head. "Read that."

"More of the Cinderfella romance between Tahira and her palace aid husband?"

"Not exactly."

With a huff, Liyah started reading, hope and despair twisting together in a knot inside her with each new paragraph. Not Cinder*fella,* but a modern-day *Cinderella* fairy tale. Where Liyah played the role of servant elevated to princess by the love of her prince.

Only Sayed *didn't* love her and he had to be furious about this. "Oh, my gosh…what are we going to do? How did they learn my name? Can we get a retraction printed?"

"And what are they to retract? The picture of us in obvious afterglow, or the speculation that Tahira and my stars did not cross because we both had different destinies?"

"Um, well…how furious are your parents about this?"

"Father is surprisingly prosaic and Mother is thrilled all her plans for a royal wedding won't be wasted."

Liyah jumped up like there was a spring under her behind. "Married?" she screeched.

Sayed winced, but then he smiled. "Under that buttoned-down exterior, you're an emotional firecracker, aren't you?"

"Don't tease me. This is too serious."

An arrested expression came over his face. "Yes, you're right. It is."

"What do you mean?" Had he changed his mind already?

He pulled her to him and leaned down to kiss her softly. "Think about it, will you do that for me?"

"Marriage?" she asked, afraid to believe.

"Yes." He kissed her again, as if he couldn't help himself. "Until tonight."

"What's happening tonight?"

"We're having dinner."

"Don't we have dinner every night?" He smiled indulgently like she'd said something sweetly funny. "Tonight's dinner will be special."

"Why?"

"I'm going to ask you a question and if you give me the right answer I'll show you the secret passage and the hidden room my great-great-grandfather built for trysts with his wife."

"Don't you mean his mistress?"

"No. He was a romantic and wanted to give her a very special wedding gift."

"So, he built a hidden room."

"Yes."

"No wonder."

"What?" Sayed asked.

"You're so incredible." She smiled up at him. "It's in the genes."

"I tried to tell you."

"So, you're going to ask me a question tonight?"

"Yes."

"Even though I'm not a princess?"

"I have told you many times, I esteem *you* highly. If I mistook what was required of me and that hurt you, I am truly sorry, but I have not wanted you out of my sight since the first time my gaze fell on you."

"You don't mean that."

"I do."

Man, he really wanted her. Like, a lot.

"You promise?"

"You have my word as emir of Zeena Sahra and *your man*."

"Sayed…" She reached up and kissed him with every bit of pent-up emotion inside her.

He picked her up with an arm under her bottom and another against her back for stability, carrying her into the bedroom without breaking their locked lips.

He loomed over her on the bed. "We are not supposed to do this here."

"You're better at breaking rules than you give yourself credit for." His mother had been right. Sayed did have a wide streak of impetuousness.

He gave her that smile again. "It's you, you're very good at tempting me to break them, *habibti*."

"Well, I may have gone to a little extra trouble with my appearance today."

He laughed, the sound so free and happy it filled her own heart with joy. "No need, you are always gorgeous to me. But I do like this dress on you."

"It's a *dishdasha*," she teased.

"Oh, is it? Pardon me."

She grinned. "It might be just as pretty off."

"Doubtful. You, on the other hand, will be infinitely more accessible naked and nothing is more beautiful to me than your body."

"Don't say things like that."

"Why not?"

"I'll believe them."

He cupped her face in his big hands. "I will never lie to you, on my honor."

Too choked to speak, she nodded.

They spent the next minutes undressing between drugging kisses.

She made a sound of victory when he was down to his sexy black silk knit boxers.

He laughed, his hands already busy on her skin.

"You wear more layers than me," she told him. "I think there's something wrong with that."

"The challenge will prevent you from becoming bored."

"Right, because you aren't challenging enough."

He proved just how challenging he could be... to her self-control, drawing forth the response her body would only ever give to this man. For the first time, there was no bitter in the sweet of that knowledge, either.

He made love to her with passion that felt as driven by the sense of reprieve as her own. Could that be possible?

He certainly hadn't seemed to be upset about the idea of marriage. Though they'd barely talked about it.

Rational thought fled as he drove her arousal higher. Unwilling to be outdone, she did her best to touch him in all the ways she knew drove him crazy.

Their coupling was powerful and intensely intimate, their bodies so in tune for the moments leading up to and during her climax, she felt like they were sharing the same soul.

CHAPTER THIRTEEN

HAVING LEARNED OF Sayed's intention to take Liyah out to dinner, Queen Durrah showed up with an ornate crimson *dishdasha* for Liyah to wear.

"But this is the color of the royal family."

"Yes, my dear, it is. It is also the gown I wore for the formal announcement of my own upcoming nuptials."

Liyah put her hands up as if warding off an attack from the dress. "I can't wear it, what if I tear it or spill something on it?"

"Don't be silly, Aaliyah," the queen said with amusement. "If I had had a daughter, she would have worn this gown to her first formal function when she came of age. It pleases me for you to wear it now."

Tears burned in Liyah's eyes.

The queen tsked and patted Liyah's cheek softly. "None of that now. I'm going to be very happy to welcome you into our family, *ya 'eni*."

"Mom used to call me that," Liyah admitted emotionally.

"Then it will be an honor for you to allow me to do so now. Just as you were the precious in your mother's eyes, you will always be in mine, as well."

The endearment literally meant *my eye,* but it carried more the connotation the queen gave it. And it touched Liyah deeply.

"You should be angry at me."

"No, Aaliyah," Queen Durrah said with certainty. "I have seen more life in my son in the past week than for two decades. You are so good for him. How could I be anything but happy at the idea of you becoming my daughter?"

"He hasn't asked me yet."

"He will."

"It's really special, you know?"

"What?"

"That he insists on asking. For all intents and purposes he's been trapped into this, but he's not treating it like a business proposal."

"All of the men of this family have a romantic streak. They always have had. I should have realized there was a problem when Sayed's showed no sign of coming out with Tahira," the queen mused.

"He told me about the hidden room."

"I always loved that story. I wanted Falah to

build me a room, but he told me it had already been done."

"Not so romantic, then." But then a king had to have a practical streak, just like a prince.

"Well…actually…"

"Oh, tell me."

The melecha smiled with obviously fond reminiscence. "He took me to a European castle for our honeymoon."

"You live in a palace."

"He bought me the castle and a title to go with it."

"Being queen wasn't enough?" Liyah teased.

"It was something that was just for me, not Zeena Sahra." Queen Durrah smiled softly. "That castle became our refuge after Umar's death, a place we could take Sayed and simply be a family."

"A place he could still be a boy and play freely," Liyah said softly.

The queen nodded. "And in safety."

Liyah was still thinking about her visit with Queen Durrah when Hasiba arrived to tell her the driver was waiting with the car.

"Where is Sayed?" Liyah asked Hasiba with some trepidation, worried the older woman would have decided Liyah took advantage again.

"I believe it is supposed to come as a surprise," Hasiba said with a conspiratorial smile.

"Okay."

Hasiba reached for Liyah before she left the suite. "I am truly sorry about before. My emir has never been so happy as since meeting you. Even back in London, though none of us understood his dreamy preoccupation was not with his coming nuptials but the woman that would steal his heart."

If only that were true. "Thank you, Hasiba. Your support means so much."

The older woman pulled Liyah into a tight hug. "You will be a wonderful emira."

Liyah would do her best.

The limo ride into the city only took about twenty minutes, but it was the longest twenty minutes of her life. It ended when they pulled up in front of an elegant hotel.

A man dressed in a dark *kameez* rushed forward to lead Liyah inside and to an old-fashioned cage elevator.

Sayed was waiting beside a table set on a dais in the center of the large and very full dining room of the hotel's rooftop restaurant.

He wore a men's *dishdasha* in the same crimson shade as Liyah's. Though with the elaborate gold embroidery on her chiffon outer dress, Liyah's was a lot fancier.

His black *abayah* had more moderate masculine embroidery in the same crimson shade. His *egal* was the ceremonial black shot with gold and his *keffiyeh* the color of the royal house, as well.

"You look like the emir," she said in a near-whisper as she took his hand to step up on the dais.

"But you remember always the man underneath the robes," he said with pure satisfaction.

"Yes."

His smile was blinding as he helped her into her chair.

Dinner was amazing, Sayed in top form, practically oozing charm.

Though they consumed no alcohol, she felt tipsy on hope by the time dessert arrived. Several photographs had already been taken throughout the evening, everyone at the tables around them smiling and nodding as if they were as much a part of what was to come as Liyah and Sayed.

Maybe they were.

Sayed would always serve his people with his whole heart.

Sayed waited until the dessert dishes had been taken away before he rose from his chair only to drop to one knee beside hers.

Even knowing he was prompted by the need to prevent more scandal, and maybe save some face in the wake of Tahira's defection, Liyah was overwhelmed with emotion.

"Aaliyah Amari, will you do me the very great honor of agreeing to become my emira and lead the people of Zeena Sahra by my side?"

His words put the weight of reality on this fantasy moment. Sayed was putting more trust in her than she could imagine. He wasn't just asking because it was expedient.

He had to believe in Liyah as a person to trust her with the position of his emira, much less his wife.

"Liyah?" he prompted softly, typically not sounding worried, but patient.

She smiled, feeling the hot track of tears on her cheeks. She hadn't even known she was crying. "Yes, oh, yes, Sayed. I want that more than anything."

"I am so pleased." Then showing the influence of many years spent living in the States, he leaned forward and sealed the deal with a kiss.

The restaurant erupted into applause, camera flashes going from phones as well as reporters strategically waiting in the wings.

Liyah didn't care. If sharing her life with Sayed meant sharing it with the rest of the world, too, then so be it.

As he leaned back, she whispered quietly for

his ears alone, "I love you. I just thought you should know."

His dark eyes heated and filled with definite pleasure. "Thank you. I will always treasure that gift."

She hadn't expected him to return the words. Liyah knew Sayed didn't love her, but his genuine appreciation of her feelings gave her hope for the future and certainty that even if he never fell in love with her, she would always have his regard and consideration.

This man would always be faithful—his "three-year drought" proved that—but just as importantly, he valued her affection. He would not take Liyah's love for granted, even if he never returned it.

Sayed waited for the video call to connect. He'd sent Yusuf to London the day before with an envelope to deliver to Gene Chatsfield.

The call connected and Gene's distinguished features filled Sayed's screen. "Sheikh Sayed, to what do I owe this pleasure?"

"Yusuf has delivered my package."

"If you mean this…" The older man lifted the heavy-duty envelope sealed with Sayed's royal family symbol set in crimson wax. "Yes."

"Inside you will find several papers."

Gene's confusion was apparent, but he seemed

too preoccupied to be nervous. "Shall I open it, then?"

"Yes."

Gene's face paled as he read the documents in front of him. "You know where she is? My daughter?"

"So now you are claiming her?"

"Denial was a knee-jerk reaction caused by similar situations in the past, none of which ended up being what they claimed."

"You decided Aaliyah's was?"

"She left the locket. I'd given it to her mother. Nothing more than a trinket to me, but she kept it all those years and passed it on to her daughter." Gene swallowed, as if emotion was getting the best of him. "She'd left my picture behind hers. I looked when I remembered."

"If you need further proof, Aaliyah's DNA report is there, as well. Running your own will provide an undeniable match."

"You know I will, because in my position I cannot afford to take anything on word alone."

"Yes."

"But I'm confident of what the test will tell us."

"As am I."

"I would like to see my daughter," Gene said with hope. "Is she working for you now?"

"We are getting married next month."

"What? How is that possible? Is she pregnant?"

"No, she does not yet carry my child. As to how and why, you do not have a place in her life that affords you personal answers of that nature."

A practical man of the world, Gene didn't flinch at the reminder. "I would like to."

"You will have to apologize," Sayed warned.

"Of course."

Sayed wasn't prepared to let it go at that. "Well enough that she believes you are sincere."

"Whatever you may think of me, my children matter to me."

"You will get one opportunity to prove that."

"And if I don't to your satisfaction, I never see my daughter again?"

"You are a man of discernment."

"And you have a reputation for ruthlessness. Does Aaliyah know that, I wonder?"

"She loves me despite my flaws." The satisfaction he felt saying those words was immense.

"I'm very glad to hear that."

"Really?"

"I would not like to think my daughter was marrying for anything but honest emotion and hope for a future."

"Come to Zeena Sahra and tell her that."

"When?"

"Yusuf is waiting to take you to our jet."

"You expect me to drop everything and come now?" Gene asked, showing dismay for the first time.

"Yes. You may bring your fiancé."

The older man waved that off. "She is busy with wedding preparations."

"Then it is the ideal time for you to make this trip."

"You don't lack arrogance, do you?"

"Aaliyah will tell you I do not."

Gene smiled. "Give me a couple of days and I will fly out commercial."

"No. Your visit must be kept under wraps. Your place in Aaliyah's life will not be announced until if and when she is prepared to recognize you as her father."

"I cannot come on a moment's notice."

"With Giatrakos at the helm? I think you can."

Gene frowned. "Fine. She deserves a little sacrifice on my part."

"More than a little, I think, but luckily for you she has me now and no *major* sacrifices on your part will be necessary."

"You called my father?" Aaliyah jumped up and paced across his mother's receiving room. "And he's going to be here within the hour?"

"Give or take, yes."

"But why?"

"Because you deserve an apology for his idiocy."

"What did you threaten him with to force the apology?" she asked suspiciously.

"No threats were required. He was already trying to find you."

"Is that what he told you?"

"Yes."

"I doubt it."

"I'd already hired a private detective and have the retainer receipt and first reports to prove it," Gene Chatsfield said, having entered the room with Yusuf through the side entrance, indicating the bodyguard had brought him into the palace discreetly. "How he missed your location when your engagement is all over the media, I don't know."

Aaliyah spun around to face her father, her face blanching before her expression turned wooden.

Sayed crossed the room and put his arm around her waist. "All will be well. You are not alone."

Gene smiled at them. "You look very good together."

"Why are you here?" Aaliyah asked baldly.

"I owe you an apology. I should have heard you out to begin with, but I'm a suspicious man. I made mistakes in the past and they made me vulnerable to a certain type of people. You were not like them, but I was blinded to that at first."

Sayed was impressed with the older man's openness and sincerity.

Aaliyah didn't look quite as taken with her father's words. "So, you acknowledge I'm your daughter now?" she asked suspiciously.

"Oh, yes."

"Don't you want a DNA test, or something?"

Gene glanced at Sayed and then back to Aaliyah. "Already done. Your fiancé provided your results."

"From the blood test?" Aaliyah asked quietly.

"Yes."

She scanned his face, as if looking for something. "You planned this."

"I did."

"What if he'd kept acting like a bastard about it?" she asked, her vulnerability to that eventuality in her tone.

Though Sayed doubted anyone else would have heard it.

He let her see how serious he was before he promised, "I would have ruined him and destroyed the Chatsfield from London to Sydney."

"Wow."

Sayed guided her to a seat on one of the small sofas and indicated a chair for her father to take. Once they were all seated, Gene said, "I realize I have a lot of making up to do to build a relationship, but I want to try."

Aaliyah looked up at Sayed. "Is he sincere or is this because I'm going to marry a prince, a pretty ruthless one at that?"

"He is sincere. Believe it."

She nodded. "Okay." Then turned her head to face Gene. "We can work on it."

"You are very forgiving. I am not sure I deserve it."

"I'm pretty sure you don't," Aaliyah said with her usual honesty.

Gene winced. "Touché."

"But Mom wanted me to try, and if you're willing, I am, too. For her sake."

"Thank you."

"I'm not calling you Dad, though."

"No, I imagine we will suffice with Gene and Aaliyah."

"Liyah. My friends call me Liyah."

"I thought Sheikh Sayed called you Aaliyah."

"Only my family calls me that."

Like his parents and him. Sayed smiled.

"And I'm not that." Gene sounded sad.

"Not yet."

"It is something you will work on," Sayed added.

The older man nodded. "Yes, I will. Liyah, I appreciate your willingness to try to forgive me—however, this news will come as a great shock to the children. I want to introduce you to them with the respect you deserve. But at the moment they are scattered throughout the world. They have lessons to learn," he said ruefully, "hard lessons to learn before I would like you to meet them. Myself and Giatrakos are working on it, and they'll all be back together soon. But for now, I would hope that you understand my request to wait."

He was only able to stay one night, but in the time he was at the palace, Gene Chatsfield had shown nothing but genuine desire to build a relationship with the daughter he hadn't known about.

Sayed was glad when both his parents confirmed his instincts that said bringing Gene Chatsfield into Aaliyah's life was the right thing to do.

He returned Aaliyah's locket to her before he left for the airport.

"That was kind of incredible," she said after waving her father off.

"I am glad you enjoyed your time with him."

"He's not nearly the jerk I thought he was."

Sayed agreed. "Just a man with fears and worries like anyone else."

"You know he offered me an equal trust

fund to what my half siblings have been given," Aaliyah informed him.

Sayed had expected something like that and would have been disappointed if Gene had not done so. "What did you say?"

"No."

"Good." He'd expected that, as well.

Aaliyah smiled. "I don't need his money. I never did."

"You just wanted family and now you have mine."

"It's a pretty wonderful family."

"My mother and father will be pleased to hear you say so."

She frowned up at him as they walked back into the palace. "You're not going to try some kind of intervention with the Amaris, are you?"

Sayed shook his head. "Absolutely not. If you were not good enough to recognize before becoming emira, they will not be allowed to claim you now."

She nodded decisively. "Good."

"Besides, if we had any of the Amaris in hitting distance, I'm not sure my mother could control herself."

Aaliyah laughed. "Now, that would make an interesting picture for the front page."

"No doubt. Let's avoid it, shall we?"

"Your mom calls me her daughter. I like it."

"So does she."

His father was extremely fond of Aaliyah, as well, but then so was Sayed. More than he'd ever thought he could feel for someone not born into his family.

He wasn't sure he was in love with her, though he thought he might be. Until he knew for certain, he wasn't saying anything. She deserved truth, not confusion.

Aaliyah's wedding was a royal *event*, attended by dignitaries, heads of state, sheikhs, other royals and European nobility.

But she was most pleased by her father and his fiancée's presence. Aaliyah's only other personal guest was Stephanie Carter, the head housekeeper from the Chatsfield San Francisco, a woman Hena Amari had called friend.

Aaliyah wore white, her dress a traditional Middle Eastern ensemble designed by a prominent Italian designer who had designed several gowns for Queen Durrah. Sayed wore a more ornate version of the outfit he'd proposed to her in.

His coronation took place directly after their wedding, though it wasn't the one everyone had been expecting. Sayed was given the distinction of crown prince, but his father had decided he wasn't ready to retire.

In fact, Sayed had shared with Liyah that

King Falah had liked the idea of training his nephew to take Sayed's place as emir before he was crowned melech. She hadn't been surprised, though she didn't tell Sayed so.

She'd had her own little talk with her soon-to-be father-in-law about the timetable for Liyah becoming melecha. She'd let him know in no uncertain terms she wasn't ready yet.

He'd taken it in good humor, and though he'd blustered a bit, he'd given in pretty easily with her idea of training Bilal to follow in Sayed's place.

The entire country celebrated the wedding and crown prince coronation into the early hours of the morning.

Following the pattern he'd established with her, Sayed lifted Liyah into his arms at the reception in the main ballroom and proceeded to carry her up the stairs and down unfamiliar corridors, ending up in his room.

"Our room now," he said as he lowered her to stand beside the bed.

"Yes, our room."

"Tonight, I make love to my emira." The expression in his dark eyes took her breath away.

She reached up and touched his face, loving the fact she was the only woman besides his mother in the entire country allowed such familiarity. "Whatever we are outside that door, when we are together intimately, you are always my *man, ya habibi,* and I will always be first and foremost your woman."

His expression turned nearly beatific. "Yes. I do. I am certain of it."

"What?" she asked, feeling like she'd missed something.

"I love you, *habibti.* I was not certain because I've never experienced anything like what you make me feel, but my heart is yours, from the moment our eyes met unto eternity."

She stopped, her heart going so fast she heard the rush in her ears. "You love me?"

"Yes. It happened so quickly, but you are perfect for me. Everything about you matches something in me."

"I'll never have a pedigree."

"And I thank God for it. You help me to see with my heart, not my position."

"I wasn't born to be a princess."

"But you were, born to be *my* emira."

She was out of arguments. "I love you, too, Sayed, so much."

"One day, you *will* carry my child."

"Yes. You'll be such a wonderful father."

"I had a very good example, just as you did for being mother to our children."

"We went from single to plural pretty fast."

"I've got a dream."

"Of lots of babies?" she asked a little worried.

"Not lots, just maybe four?"

"Four? Wow, you do realize I was an only child, right?"

"But you have so much love to give."

That was one truth she could no longer deny. Gone were the days when Liyah denied her emotions. "You're being persuasive again."

He turned and grabbed something off the bed and handed it to her. "Thank you for marrying me."

She smiled and stepped back from the box. "Just a second."

She'd asked Hasiba to make sure Liyah's gift for Sayed had been dropped off in the suite. She found it on the desk, wrapped in burgundy paper, the royal crest holding the gold ribbon together instead of a bow.

She rushed back into the room and offered it to him. "Thank *you* for marrying me."

"Your love is all the gift I need," he said fervently.

"Ditto."

He smiled and opened the gift, his expression going very solemn as he opened the jeweler's box. It was a traditional wedding bracelet, of the type brides gave their husband in Zeena

Sahra. Though it was not leather, or hand woven from her hair.

It had something to do with their Bedouin roots, but all Liyah knew was that she approved the symbolism of it.

"The eternal circle of love and commitment," Sayed said with satisfaction.

"Yes, because I will always love you and am in this thing for life."

"As am I." He slipped the heavy platinum masculine bracelet on, a single ruby for his royal house offset left of center on the top.

She'd used the last of her savings to buy it and couldn't think of a better use of her mother's final gift to Liyah.

"Now it is your turn."

"Is it?" she asked, so full of love and happiness she didn't think any gift could add to it.

"Yes. I remember you once told me, we are supposed to keep things even."

She laughed, remembering. "That was about getting naked."

"We will get to that."

"Promise?" she teased.

"Oh, yes. Now, open your gift."

Liyah tore the paper off the flat box and pulled off its lid, but was a little confused when she saw it was filled with legal documents. "What are these?"

"You know the hotel where I proposed?"

"Yes." She'd loved the rooftop restaurant.

"I bought it for you."

"You bought me a hotel?"

"It's in your blood, but you'll have to keep a general manager as your duties as emira will not allow for a full-time occupation outside of the palace."

"Your mother explained." Queen Durrah had been giving Liyah "princess lessons" daily since she agreed to marry Sayed.

"And you do not mind?"

"No, Sayed. When I say I love you, I mean the you that is emir, too."

"You are amazing, *habibti. Intee albi.*"

"And you are my heart. We'll beat for each other. I love you so much, Sayed."

"As I love you. With everything that I am or ever will be."

"I know it."

"You do?"

"The proof is in the pudding, as they say." Her heart was so full it was hard to get the words out, but she did. "First you gave me the gift of family, both my father and your own parents, cousins and aunt. Then there's the hotel—the grand romantic gesture the men in your family are known for."

"I should have realized I loved you when I started negotiations for the hotel."

"Maybe."

"Perhaps you need a little more proof." Sayed's meaning was clear in the hunger glowing in his espresso eyes.

"I'll never say no to that type of proof."

Nor would she ever balk at giving it. Love had turned her from repressed into passionately expressive.

And Sayed adored her that way. He said so.

They made love throughout the night, taking turns expressing their spiritual affection in carnal ways no less beautiful than the emotion that flowed between them.

Ultimately, Hena Amari had gifted Liyah with Sayed, her final request leading her daughter to London where fate ordained she connect with the other half of her soul.

Liyah whispered a prayer of gratitude as she slipped into sleep, wrapped in the arms of her one true love, and hoped her mother could hear it, as well.

* * * * *

If you enjoyed this book, look out for the next instalment of THE CHATSFIELD: *PLAYBOY'S LESSON by Melanie Milburne, coming next month.*